The Realm of Districts

Andrew Zellgert

Zellgertbooks

Contents

This story is dedicated to a daisy I found in a field

and the adventures that followed because of it.

Hello

H ello there, stranger.

I know what you're thinking. Oh no, it's another story that starts with a mysterious voice; how dull! I promise you; this story is different. The tale I'm about to tell is a story that happened to me a long time ago. Back when the mining facilities of the south were still in operation, and the lands were covered in darkness.

But for me to recount everything properly, I must first introduce myself. My name is Alex. I was one of many slaves trapped within the Realm of Districts before the engines echoed and the—What? What do you mean you've never heard of the Realm of Districts?

Have you ever?

Well, before I tell you that story, I should first recount what happened before. After all, knowing the past can often assist with predicting the future and the repercussions that come along with it.

So, pull up a chair and grab a snack! It all started a long time ago in a forgotten age of adventure and peril.

This is the Tale of the Realm of Districts.

Chapter One

Welcome To Normal

Alex walked across the busy subterranean walkways. Bustling workers and employees of all shapes and sizes could be seen wearing their hard hats, drenched in sweat, as they walked under the flickering incandescents. Holographic advertisements flashed across the walls, recommending that the workers stop by various locations and grab something to eat.

Alex cut ahead of a couple of her fellow coworkers and made her way up a flight of slimy stone steps and onto a landing covered in metal grates. Steam hissed, and fires roared as the young woman marched alongside the overlook. Tapping her hand against the guard rails as she went.

"Hey, Alex! How's it going today?" asked a young man as he smiled widely and patted Alex on the back.

Alex smiled widely and replied, "Going great, Fred!"

"Check this out!" said Fred excitedly. He rolled up his sleeve to reveal a massive bloody gash in his arm. "I'm going to the medical ward to have this cleaned up! Wish me luck!"

Alex nodded enthusiastically and waved back as Fred walked off down the hall, smiling and laughing. He didn't seem disturbed by the nasty wound in his arm in the slightest. Nobody seemed concerned about his wound at all, Alex included. Everyone was smiling. That's all the workers knew how to do in District 10 even if they didn't feel it within.

"All workers, please be sure to clock in with your worker ID before proceeding through the terminal," said a robotic voice over the intercom.

Alex nodded with a smile and swiped her red worker card into a reader, and the doors opened, letting her pass through into the mining room. Various metal shafts and gears turned aggressively, causing deafening clacking sounds to echo throughout the metal room as the sounds of pickaxes and furnace fires roared.

"Hey Alex!" said one of the workers, who almost leapt over to where she stood. "Ariana died today!"

"Oh really?" asked Alex excitedly. "How did she die?"

"She got torn to shreds by one of the cogs!" said the other, and they both laughed together.

"That sounds about right!" said a third employee excitedly, who walked over to them.

"So, what's on the agenda for today?" asked Alex as she looked around at the smoke and machinery around her.

"We need to spend twelve hours shoveling coal into this furnace!" replied the man in charge. He wore a tweed jacket with a bowler hat and a bushy black mustache that curled on the ends. He seemed out of place in a factory setting, but nobody raised any objection to his presence within the facility.

Alex saluted the man, and she shoveled coal into the furnaces and continued to keep the fires burning. Hour after hour after hour, she shoveled. Continuing the grueling cycle of shovel, lift, drop. Shovel, lift, drop. Shovel, lift, drop. Her arms screamed at her, begging her to stop, but she didn't listen. They always did that.

"Oops!" said a voice with a laugh.

"What is it?" asked Alex as she shoveled her pile of coal.

"Jerry fell in!" said a miner as he limped his way over to peer into the furnace. "I guess he's gone now!"

They chuckled some more, and they fueled the furnace for the remainder of the shift.

"All workers, please be sure to clock out with your worker ID before proceeding through the terminal to your dorms," said a robotic voice over the intercom.

"That was fun!" said Fred as he shook his bloody arm.

"How was the medical ward?" asked Alex as they walked toward the terminal with their ID cards.

"They told me to deal with it," replied Fred with a laugh. "They told me I imagined the pain. It is all inside your head anyway, so it doesn't matter!"

"Interesting!" said Alex with a laugh as she skipped down the subterranean tunnel and out into a massive clearing in a cavern stretching as far as the eye could see. A bustling city filled with flying cars and laughing people. A city where violence was laughed at and considered normal. Where death wasn't just common, it was expected. Welcome to normal. Welcome to District 10.

The residents of District 10 were oblivious to how brainwashed they truly were. Not realizing that the advertisements and employers were lying to them. Not realizing that what they had come to expect as normal was not normal but rather warped and distorted.

Alex continued skipping down the cobblestone streets, up a slight incline and into a massive boxy building made of red brick. Up a flight of stairs and down the hall until she made it to her dorm. She swiped her card and entered the room comprised of a desk, a bed, and her sleeping apparatus. Every night, if there even were such a thing, the residents of District 10 would wear these to help them fall asleep. The device was said to 'interface with the brain to assist with REM sleep.' And the workers believed this lie to a t.

Alex put her sleeping apparatus on and drifted into her forced REM where she dreamed about allegiance to District 10 and her desire to work until she collapsed. As the residents of Alex's dorm complex continued to sleep, one person was still stirring. An older man with sagging skin and graying hair. This man's name was John, and he was Alex's dorm neighbor. He had been in District 10 for a long time and had learned many things during his time as a worker. He reached between his mattress cushions, pulled out a small leather book and dusted it off carefully.

He looked to the left, then to the right, then made a break for it.

Out of the dorm and down the hall, he ran past workers turning in for their 'nightly' rest and past dorm housekeepers.

"Hey, John!" smiled one housekeeper brightly. "How's your work going?"

"It's going fine," replied John with a forced smile as he carefully slipped around her and down a flight of stairs. The housekeeper cocked her head as she followed John down the steps.

"I said, hey, John!" she said with a wider smile as she reached out a hand for the older man.

"Not you, too," muttered the older man. "Ack. I should have known."

"Why aren't you smiling, John?" asked the housekeeper as she ominously approached the older man with her arms outstretched, her smile widening further beyond imagining.

"Stay away from me, you freak!" yelled John. He bolted down the stairs, and the housekeeper's smile reached the breaking point. She yelled, "Maintenance evacuation procedure! All workers evacuate the building now. We have scheduled maintenance to perform!"

In an instant, the sleep apparatuses' released, the workers got up in unison and stepped out of their dorms, smiling widely.

"Darn," muttered John as he ran out of the brick building and out onto the streets, missing the sea of evacuating workers only by moments.

"All workers, please be sure to clock in with your worker ID before proceeding through the terminal to your dorms," said the robotic intercom.

"Screw your terminals," murmured John as he kept running as fast as his legs could go clutching the small leather book to his chest as hard as he could.

"Why aren't you smiling?" asked a worker as they approached John.

"Listen to me, all of you!" yelled John as he held up the book. "I've found hope! Hope for all of you if you would only listen! There is a way out of this prison!" He held the book up for all to see. "Please!" A small crowd gathered as the workers funneling out of the dorms found themselves face to face with John and his small book. "This book has all of the answers!"

"Everyone step aside," said a voice with a chuckle, and the crowd parted to reveal the man with the tweed jacket and bowler hat.

John lowered the book and held it tightly against his chest. "What do you want?" he asked coldly.

"Now, now. Let's not be a downer!" said the man as he twirled his mustache.

"I know what this place is, you psycho," said John as he clenched the book tighter. "I also know what you're building. When the King hears about this…"

"You're not going anywhere," said the man in the hat with a smile that lacked warmth or love of any kind. "You work for me, and that is how it is going to be."

"You want to play this in front of all your precious workers?" said John. "Let's see how long you can hide the truth from them. You can't do this forever."

The man in the bowler hat punched John square in the face, and he fell backward over the edge and out of sight. The crowd laughed as they watched him fall to his death with a heavy thud. Maybe it was fate, perhaps it was destiny, but the leather book flew into the air and out of sight.

"Now, everyone, get back to work!" said the man in the bowler hat. "You will have your sleep time later. Chop chop!"

Alex nodded and made her way back toward the subterranean tunnel. They all journeyed down back toward the engine room, laughing and smiling with one another. The run-in with John and the bowler hat superior didn't seem to faze anyone in the slightest. Nor the idea that they had witnessed a murder. Everything was back to how it was, except for an important thing.

The book was nowhere to be seen, and Alex was no longer smiling.

Chapter Two

The Joyous Railroad

"**A**ll workers, please be sure to clock in with your worker ID before proceeding through the terminal," said the robotic intercom.

Alex looked around at her fellow workers uneasily as she tried to stay calm. She felt as though she had woken up after a long sleep, and the horrors of her reality were finally being identified. She felt the book pressed warmly against her chest, almost as if it were comforting her.

Voices filled her mind, whispering words such as, "The shepherd will leave the 99 for the one." And "He always keeps his promises."

Fred ran up to Alex, and the young woman jumped out of her skin.

"Hey Alex!" said Fred with a laugh as he showed his bloody arm to her, and Alex froze. "Look at this! The medical ward gave me stitches!"

Alex stared, petrified at the wounded arm and the needles and thread sticking out at odd ends. Clumsily stitched together like a child who played with a sewing machine.

"Isn't this great?" said Fred excitedly, and Alex shook her head.

Fred cocked his head and smiled wider. "What's the matter, Alex? Isn't this funny?"

"No, Fred. It's not," she whispered.

Fred's smile widened.

The voices in her mind amplified. "For he so loved the world he gave his one and only son."

"Are you alright, Alex?" he asked with a loud, false laugh, and Alex backed away from her so-called friend.

The voices began to swirl around her mind.

"Run, Alex."

"Your time has come."

"You must leave."

Alex's retreat quickened.

"Are you sure everything's alright, Alex?" said Fred with his arms outstretched. He advanced toward her as a crowd gathered hoping to witness another murder.

"Stay away from me, Fred," mumbled Alex. She didn't know what was happening or why. All she knew was this place she called home made her sick, and she wanted to leave with the mysterious mind-voices.

Fred's face distorted, and a black mustache formed across his upper lip, and he withdrew a bowler hat and put it atop his head. His worker's uniform contorted into a tweed jacket, and Alex immediately recognized him not for who he seemed to be, but what he was. She watched the man as he leered at her and twirled his mustache.

"How interesting," he whispered as he looked her up and down, a streak of firelight across his eyes as he spoke.

The crowd laughed. How did they not find this alarming?

"You must've found John's book. Throw it on the ground, and it will be properly disposed of."

"No," murmured Alex as she stepped backward.

"Hmmm," replied the man. He reached a hand out toward her while his tongue slipped in and out. "Don't you want to keep working for me? I can give you what you desire."

Clouds shrouded Alex's vision, and various silhouettes danced around her. One of a couple kissing. The man was wearing a handsome tuxedo, and the woman an ornate dress with her hair curled neatly. Alex squinted and realized the woman was her kissing the man. How beautiful she looked and to be with such a handsome person. Her heart filled with longing as she reached out toward the silhouette. She wanted to be loved. She felt a void in her heart she had never felt before, and she desired romance more than ever.

She stared at the man as he pushed her hair behind her ears and held her close. She wanted to be with him.

Ding, Ding, Ding, Ding, Ding.

The faint sounds of a railroad gate alarm ringing could be heard as faint pricks of flashing red could be seen off in the distance, but Alex paid no attention to this.

"Hmmm," said the man as he drifted around her like smoke. "You can be with him if you wish. You can be as beautiful as she. All you need to do is throw the book down."

Alex felt the book in her hands grow warmer as it tried to comfort her. She wanted to be beautiful, and this man was offering her this nice deal. To be with someone so handsome and to have companionship.

"Now, the book," hissed the man as he twirled his mustache and flicked his tongue. His eyes hungrily stared at the book as Alex slowly withdrew it and held it up. The man backed away slightly as the book came near him almost as if the book were a burning flame. Alex held the book above her head and loud train whistle cut through the silence and a massive white light blasted through the smoke and the man leapt out of the way.

"Oy!" yelled a voice as a steam train approached faster and faster. "Did you flag us?"

"I think she did, Matthew! Why else do you think she raised the book?"

"Well, let's waste no time then!" said the first. There came a hearty laugh, and, in an instant, Alex was picked up by the passing train and the mustached man ran after them. His tweed jacket billowing violently as the train came crashing through the subterranean tunnel. "Get back here!" he growled.

"Sorry folks!" said a man in a blue conductor's uniform. "Train coming through!"

Alex looked around at the piping and industrial parts throughout the cabin as the conductor and an engineer carefully pulled levers and turned knobs letting steam in and out of specific areas within the engine.

CHOOOOOOOOOOO!!!!!

The train let out a massive whistle as it passed by workers within District 10.

"Everyone out of the way!" said the conductor as he bit into a sandwich with a cheesy smile. "Don't worry! Things will get cheddar!"

"Oh, you and your cheese puns!" said the engineer as he pulled levers and the engines hissed.

"They look very Swiss-picious," said the conductor, and they all laughed as the train continued to rocket its way down the tunnel.

Alex watched the awestruck workers as they stared at the massive steam train.

"It's unfortunate they will forget this ever happened as soon as we leave," replied the engineer grimly. "But we can't do anything for them unless they take the first step."

"Yeah," sighed the conductor as he closed the window. He bit into his sandwich again and turned to Alex. "So, where are you heading?"

Alex opened her mouth to speak, but no words came out. The voices had returned to her mind, and she didn't know what to do about it.

"Let me try," said the engineer over his shoulder. "¿adónde vas?"

Alex stared at him blankly.

"Où vas-tu?

Wohin gehst du?

Dove stai an—"

"I speak English," mumbled Alex, and the engineer stopped talking.

"Well, that's cleared up; where is your destination?" asked the conductor kindly.

"I'm not entirely sure," replied Alex. "I just know I don't want to be in District 10 anymore."

"I see," replied the conductor. "Are you on a mission? If so, we can drop you off wherever you wish."

"I honestly don't know anywhere outside of District 10," insisted Alex.

"I see," murmured the conductor as he pulled a lever, and they blasted through the wall of the subterranean tunnel and into a swirling white cosmic tunnel. "In that case, would you like to consult a map? We have a map car filled with schematics if you wish to view them."

Alex nodded, and she gratefully followed the conductor out of the engine room, down a couple of cargo cars, and into an ornate room filled with hand-drawn maps, compasses, and various writing utensils.

"We are currently here," he said as he pointed to a massive black patch on the map labeled 'District 10.' He chuckled to himself and murmured, "The belly of the beast."

Alex gazed at the other locations on the map, and bands surrounded District 10 in descending order. 'District 9, District 8, District 7' all the way until it reached a river labeled 'Serenity Channel.' Beyond this were many villages and settlements, with one great castle at the top and a moat around it, simply labeled 'Kingdom.' Between the two was a picture of a small bridge over the river labeled 'Serenity' with a road connecting Kingdom and District 1. A small marking of a tower just beyond that, like that of a lighthouse. Alex continued to curiously view the map as her nervous fingers followed all of the paths on it.

"So, were you in District 10 conducting a covert mission?" asked the conductor brightly. He put his hands in his pockets and then chuckled. "It's none of my concern. What am I saying?" He bit into his sandwich thoughtfully and watched Alex as she carefully observed the map.

"Where do you think I should go?" asked Alex hopefully.

"Well, I can't make that choice for you," said the conductor. "We bring people places, but where you go is completely up to you. Have you spoken with the King about your mission yet?"

Alex shook her head.

"Well, perhaps you should pay him a visit first!" said the conductor as he handed the map to Alex. "But first, we have to get out of this illusion. The Realm of Districts is tricky, and it is easy to get steered off the right path in such a place."

He glanced at the windows nervously and immediately lowered the shades.

"Anyway. You'd better head to your quarters. I don't know if you had any sleep in District 10, but from what

I've heard, you typically don't." He smiled at Alex, then walked back out of the map room to talk to the engineer once again.

Alex gazed at the map and studied it carefully. One moment, she was a mindless slave; now, she was free and would meet a King to tell her about a mission. Questions swam around in her mind as the train continued to rocket through the glistening white tunnel.

But for the time being, she would get some sleep. She had a massive journey ahead of her.

Chapter Three

The Quest

Despite the rattling and bumping of the steam train, Alex slept peacefully and woke up feeling refreshed. The lack of a sleeping apparatus really made a difference in the quality of her rest. As she stretched her back and looked around at her small train compartment. A gentle hiss of steam filled the air, and the train came to a stop, causing Alex to shift on the bed.

"Ladies and gentlemen, this is your conductor speaking. We are taking a brief stop in Serenity to refuel before making our way to Kingdom. Thank you for your patience."

The loudspeaker clicked off, and Alex got up and stretched. She stared at the mysterious book John had owned sitting on her nightstand and thought about it curiously. What was it for? She was about to get up to read the mysterious leather book when there came a knock, and she promptly slid her compartment door open.

On the other side was a clean-shaven man with long, flowing brown hair and an ornate smile on his face. "Hello, Alex," he said with a warm smile.

This man slightly took Alex aback and how abruptly he had appeared.

"May I come in?" he asked.

"Sure," said Alex as she gestured for the man to step inside, and he sat down in an armchair opposite her.

"I wanted to personally welcome you to Serenity Station," he said.

"Okay," replied Alex. "Thank you."

"This is the bridge that separates Kingdom from the Realm of Districts," he said thoughtfully. "This place has been here for a long time, built to allow slaves trapped in that vile web to come back to the Light and be made new." He gazed at Alex and continued, "I'm also here to discuss the finding of the Book of Wisdom." He gestured to the book sitting on the nightstand.

"Do you need it?" asked Alex.

"No, you do," replied the man as he smiled at her. His eyes dazzled with light as he spoke. "The Book of Wisdom is a very powerful book. It can provide knowledge when all you see is deception, weapons when all you see is malice, and love when it feels like there is none." He shifted in the chair then continued. "The book is a tool created by the King to aid knights such as yourself on quests."

"Knights?" asked Alex curiously.

"Indeed," replied the man thoughtfully. "You, like many others, have been assigned as warriors of the crown. Knights who go out onto the field of battle and slay the forces of evil in the name of the Kingdom."

"But I can't do that," whispered Alex as she looked around nervously. "I can barely make my own choices. I tend to overthink things. I get caught up in—"

"Peace be with you," whispered the man as he held up a hand, and Alex stopped talking.

"You are a strong warrior, Alex," he said. "You simply need to trust me." He smiled again, and Alex felt peace and joy like she had never felt before.

"So, you said I'm a knight. A warrior who goes on quests?" asked Alex.

"That is correct," replied the man. "In fact, that is why I'm here. To discuss your quest."

Alex straightened up and leaned forward attentively.

"You are familiar with the Realm of Districts, and your knowledge about such a place can be quite useful," said the man. "We need you to go back into that realm of shadows and put an end to the reign of terror those monsters have upheld for centuries. They stole that land from us, and we're going to win it back."

"Why can't you do it yourself?" asked Alex. "Surely you could with such a powerful Kingdom?"

"You are right, we could," replied the man. "But sadly, we cannot enter the Realm of Districts without someone asking us to. The reason the Joyous Express found you was because you flagged them. We can only enter there if someone truly and genuinely wants us there."

"Couldn't you take the place by force?" asked Alex, who was secretly trying to get out of the task at hand.

"We could do that too, but love that is forced upon others isn't love at all," replied the man simply. "Authentic love has to be a choice. If we marched into the Realm of Districts and attempted to force everyone to do my will, what kind of a person would I be? I'd be no better than the monsters themselves! Think about it, Alex. Love involves consent. Choosing to love another not for personal gain, but rather because you care, and you are willing to put another's needs before your own."

Alex stopped and pondered the man's words. He had a good point and there was no denying it. "You can turn the train around," she sighed. "I'll make my way back to District 10, and I'll help you win it back."

"I'm afraid it's not that simple," sighed the man. "You need to go through ALL the districts to make it back to where you were. There simply isn't anyone in that realm who wants to be rescued." He sighed heavily and said, "I hear their heart's cries. I see their deeds. I want to help them, but if they don't reach out and refuse to be rescued, I cannot do anything about it."

"Wait, so I have to go through all the districts?" asked Alex in alarm. "Why was I brought all the way here—"

"To talk with me," replied the man. "You have purpose, Alex. And I'm here to help you every step of the way. You will be challenged and pushed, but you will never be pushed beyond what you're capable of. All things are possible through me." He got up from the chair and put his hands in his pockets. "Ultimately, it's up to you. I cannot make the choice for you; however, you would be doing me a great service if you follow through with it." He reached out a hand and asked, "Will you join me?"

Alex looked up at the man. She felt safe, loved, and at peace with herself. Calm washed over her, and her heart leapt for joy as she nodded and took the man's hand and shook it firmly.

"Very good," replied the man. "The train will stop at the edge of our borders, the entrance to District 1. That is as far as the Joyous Express can take you before they run into trouble."

Alex looked up at the man and smiled. "I won't let you down."

The man nodded and made his way toward the sliding door.

"Wait, what's your name?" asked Alex.

The man turned and replied, "I am known by many names. Wonderful Counselor, teacher, savior, but you can call me Peace." Without another word, he saw himself out of Alex's quarters, and the young woman found herself alone once again. She turned to the book and opened it. Voices swirled around in her mind as her eyes scanned the pages of wisdom. The book had knowledge about anything and everything. Advice on how to battle various monsters and even what their weaknesses were. As she kept reading, she felt her heart grow fonder as her faith strengthened. The train started to move, and the voice of the conductor could be heard once again.

"Ladies and gentlemen, we are now departing Serenity station. We will be taking a slight detour to the Old Lighthouse before turning back en route to Kingdom. Again, thank you for your patience."

Alex thought to herself with a smile. The Old Lighthouse? That must be her stop. As the train bumped along the nonexistent tracks, passing Serenity station, then rushing through fields of green. The young woman gazed out the windows as the green countryside passed by. She would win this one. For the good of all. For Peace. For the Kingdom.

Chapter Four

The Inquires

The green countryside passed by as the train chugged along on its merry way, passing over a massive stone bridge with a sign stating, 'Thank you for visiting Serenity.' Strong oak trees stood tall, and babbling brooks flowed freely. It was all beautiful. A beauty Alex had never taken the time to appreciate.

"We are now approaching the Old Lighthouse. Please make your way to the front now."

Alex got up, grabbed the Book of Wisdom, and made her way down the narrow train halls toward the front. After opening up the steam engine room, she found herself face-to-face with the conductor.

"Nothing gouda happens without the light!" said the conductor as he bit into an apple with a hearty laugh. "Those monsters will be feta up with me in no time!"

"Your cheese puns are sooo terrible," said the engineer, who was practically crying with laughter, leaning up against a lever for support.

Alex chuckled to herself. The engineer and conductor turned promptly in response.

"Alright, Alex. This is your stop," said the conductor as he bit into his apple again. He gestured to a massive white lighthouse, shining a beam of vibrant white light out into the dark, murky waters ahead.

"Wait. I thought I was going to District 1?" asked Alex.

"Most of District 1 is just water," said the engineer as he carefully stood up. "Might as well be an ocean. The king positioned lighthouses at the edge of our borders to help lost sailors find their way home. Very few find the light these days." He shook his head sadly.

"According to our sources, the shortest path to land is from this lighthouse straight out," said the conductor. "We wish you all the best. May the King's love take you onward."

They saluted Alex, and she nodded in return. The young woman stepped out of the train and looked out at the misty waters stretching as far as the eye could see. The lighthouse shone brightly above her, and she turned back to the Joyous Express one last time before the steam rushed, and, in a heartbeat, the train was gone. Off on another mission, no doubt. She cautiously looked around at the landscape before her. The grass was a gradient, starting as a beautiful, lush green behind the lighthouse but slowly growing more monotone and uglier as it continued past the structure toward the water. The grass at the edge of the shore had no color at all. Alex was half convinced it was dead.

"Hello! Who goes there?" called a voice from above.

Alex looked up, and before her was a silhouette standing on the top balcony of the lighthouse, waving down to her.

"Just a moment!" called the voice.

There was a pause, then out came the most peculiar man Alex had ever met. He had two magnifying glasses duct-taped together to form a massive pair of glasses, a sailor's attire, and a telescope in his belt. The magnifying glasses made his eyes look four times bigger than they actually were, and Alex was a little startled at first when she encountered the man.

"Hello there!" said the man brightly. "My name is Watcher! What's your name?"

Alex opened her mouth, then closed it again.

"Ah, that's alright. You just need your boat rental! Follow me!" Watcher bounced his way up toward a moss-covered shed, and Alex followed close behind. After rummaging in the old shed for a moment, he dragged a small wooden boat and carefully brought it to the blackened waters. "There we are!" he said. "I know it's none of my business, but why are you venturing out this way?" He then shook his head and murmured, "Mustn't ask questions. Mustn't ask questions." He handed Alex a pair of oars and smiled at her warmly. "Good luck! Good luck! Yes, you'll need lots of luck," he whispered as he made his way back toward the lighthouse. The last thing Alex heard before the lighthouse door closed was the man call back, "Let me know if you don't die!"

Slam.

The door was closed, and Alex found herself alone, staring out at the waters of District 1 with the boat bobbing gently in the vile waters. She carefully sat down in the bumpy boat, set her book down, and pushed off the shore. Immediately, everything changed. Fog filled her vision, and despite being only a few feet away, she could not see any land. All that could be seen was the lighthouse beam cutting through the fog. Still trying to bring lost sailors home. Alex shivered and began rowing. The waters splashed up against the side of the boat, causing the icy waves of fear to trickle down her spine.

The row through District 1 was not pleasant in the slightest. She couldn't tell if she was rowing forwards or backwards, left or right. She knew she was moving somewhere but wasn't entirely certain as to where.

Slap. Slap. Slap.

Went the waves as they sloshed against the sides of the small rowboat. After what felt like hours of this monotonous routine, Alex stopped to rest her arms. They were so sore she didn't think she could row any further.

"Hello?" she cried. Only the chilling breeze and splash of the cold, unforgiving sea replied.

Black mist swirled, waves splashed, and the boat rocked. Nothing changed.

Alex sighed and put her head in her hands. What had she signed up for? She felt the Book of Wisdom slip out of her hands and land on the bottom of the boat with a thump.

She looked down at the book and reached out a hand for the leather tome. She had been told there was knowledge within this book. Maybe some knowledge would prove useful right now?

"Hello? Hello! Do you need any assistance?" called a voice off in the distance.

Alex looked up, the book for the moment forgotten, as she straightened up to see a small cluster of slimy rocks come into view. On top were many beautiful mermaids brushing each other's hair and splashing their tails in the cold water.

Alex took a moment to take in their perfect faces, flowing hair, and shimmering eyes. She longed to be beautiful like them but knew she could never achieve such a feat. They were simply better than her.

"Do you need any assistance?" asked one of the mermaids as she leapt off the rock and swam through the cold waters toward Alex's boat.

"Yes! I do! I do!" cried Alex. "I need help finding shore."

"Oh, we can help with that!" exclaimed another mermaid. "We know everything about these waters! Where do you come from?"

"I have been to many places," replied Alex as she looked around at them all with a smile. "All I need to do is to reach the shores of District 2."

The mermaids looked at each other, then whispered amongst themselves for a moment. After a moment of discourse, they all turned to Alex and smiled at her.

"Why should we trust you?" they asked.

One swam up to her and said, "We have no reason to believe a word you say. Tell us something about yourself so you can gain our trust."

"Err," replied Alex. "My name is Alex."

"What's your height?"

"I think it's 5 foot 6."

"Where were you born?"

"When were you born?"

The questions from the mermaids continued, and just when Alex thought she had answered one, another would come up, and she sat there for hours answering the mermaids' questions. She wanted such beautiful creatures to trust her. This continued on for a long time and the longer Alex talked with the mermaids, the closer the boat seemed to come toward the rock. Almost as if an unseen force were moving Alex closer toward the sea creatures.

"What is your favorite sport?"

"Your least favorite sport?"

"Favorite season?"

"Favorite hobby?"

The questions carried on still. In time, the questions began to slowly change into rather intrusive inquiries such as "How long were you in District 10? When did you encounter the King?" Alex, who at this point was almost hypnotized by the questions, honestly answered everything. The boat came closer to them until there was a gentle bump and the boat touched the rock with a soft thud.

The mermaids began to circle in on Alex as she continued to answer questions, blind to the eminent danger approaching from all around her. Fur slowly sprouted from the beautiful mermaid's skin and fangs grew ever longer within their mouths as they all turned into savage furry beasts. With savage claws and pointed ears. The mermaids almost resembled that of brown wolves than sea creatures.

The first of these beasts stepped into the boat and opened her mouth to take a bite out of Alex's head. Another step forward and the creature screamed in agony as its foot came into contact with the Book of Wisdom.

"Fool," hissed one of the beasts as Alex continued to answer the unspoken questions in her trace-like state. "She's too well protected. We're going to have to send her through."

"Why, I'm starving!" complained the first creature.

"I'm aware, but we cannot get close to her," hissed the other. "We'll tow her to District 2. They'll know what to do with her."

They all nodded knowingly and contorted back into their gorgeous mermaid states. They all dove into the waters, and as Alex continued to recite answers under their spell, they pushed her rowboat through the black waters. It took many hours of swimming, but at long last, they reached the shore, and they pulled Alex out of her trance.

"We have arrived," said one of the mermaids with a smile.

Alex looked around at the black grass along the coastline and thanked the 'mermaids' for their help, ignorant of the peril she had just avoided. She picked up the Book of Wisdom and waved goodbye to the sea creatures as they swam off.

Alex looked at the mysterious path before her. There was only one way forward, and she would give it her best. How fortunate for her there had been nothing dangerous in District 1. Just a few mermaids brushing each other's hair. She smiled to herself and skipped off down the path as the mermaids swam around toward another shore to alert the people of District 2 of an unexpected guest.

Chapter Five

Townsfolk

The dead trees of District 2 cast leafless shadows onto the barren ground. Shrieks could be heard off in the distance, and Alex nervously looked around at the devoid landscape. Her breath grew colder as she continued her way further and further from the shore. Gripping the book tightly to her chest as she continued on her journey.

The temperature dropped drastically the further she went. Faint snowflakes could be seen falling to the ground as she pressed on toward the unknown. An icy chill that wasn't coming from the weather enveloped her soul as she trudged on through the increasing snow and ice. Though the weather attacked her again and again, the warmth from the Book of Wisdom kept her safe.

She had almost given up hope when she saw smoke off in the distance and with great excitement ran toward it. Where there is smoke, there is also fire. She ran through the snow, book in hand, toward the source of the pillar of warm gas. Over another hill and she saw, nestled between two hills, a quaint little village. Smoking chimneys and orange lights in the windows could be seen even from a distance, and Alex gratefully ran toward them as fast as her legs could go. She could collect supplies in this place. She could be given shelter from the onslaught of snow and ice.

As she entered the borders of the village, two men in tuxedos approached. Despite their minimal layers and formal attire, they didn't seem cold. They looked at Alex sternly and put their hands up.

"HALT," said one.

"You are not permitted to enter," replied the other.

Alex stared at them and desperately tried to see around to the other side.

"All I need is shelter," she pleaded.

The men looked at each other, then at her book, then back to her.

"Alright," they replied. "But no funny business or we'll have you thrown out."

Alex nodded hastily and ran past them and into the closest building she could find. The warmth of a fire struck her skin, and cheery laughter could be heard around her. A bard played melodies of a forgotten time and various townsfolk raised their glasses in thanks for the music and entertainment.

"Hello, welcome to the Slanted Tavern."

Alex turned, and there, smiling back at her, was a young man who couldn't be much older than she was. The man smiled at her, and she smiled back.

"How may I help you?" inquired the man.

"Oh, I just came in from the cold," replied Alex as she shivered slightly.

The man nodded knowingly, briefly glancing at the Book of Wisdom before resuming eye contact. "I see," he replied. "Do you want anything to eat?"

Alex nodded enthusiastically, and the man put his hands in his pockets, walked behind a wooden counter and looked up at her expectantly.

"I'll have bread?" she asked awkwardly.

"Very well. 4.50," said the man as he scribbled a couple of calculations on a sheet of parchment.

Alex sighed. She had no money. She set her book down and pretended to reach into her pockets, but the man interrupted.

"Tell you what. I'll make an exception. Just because you're here from the storm." He scratched out the calculation, bagged a warm, steaming loaf and handed the bag to Alex.

He smiled at her warmly and waved goodbye as she walked over to an oak table and carefully opened the bag. She could tell the man was still watching her, but she ignored him as best as she could. Everyone seemed interested in her book, and she would not let anyone steal it.

"Ello, miss," came a gruff voice. Alex slowly turned, and to her horror, a man with a scraggly black beard was sitting next to her. Scars covered his older face, and an eyepatch covered an eye that had seen combat in ways Alex preferred not to think about.

"Hi," replied Alex shortly.

"That's some book you got there," the man said as his good eye stared at her intensely.

"Yeah," came another voice. Alex looked up, and another man with a brown beard approached and sat down on her other side. A silver shimmering hook was on one of his hands. Pirates.

"Yeah, it's a nice book," replied Alex uneasily. "I'm trying to eat. Could you sit somewhere else?"

"Arr. I'd prefer to sit here," replied 'Eyepatch' shortly. "Men, take a look at this young lass."

A couple more pirates joined Alex's table, and they all gawked at her book and stared at her hungrily.

One pirate reached out to take the book, but Alex picked it up and pressed it against her chest. "This is my book. Leave me alone."

"Ah ha ha ha," said Eyepatch as he scooted a little closer to Alex. "We'd be willing to provide you with proper winter gear in exchange for that tome that sits before ye."

Alex shook her head.

"A stubborn one, eh?" asked 'brown beard', and the pirates snickered.

"Indeed," replied Eyepatch. His good eye rolled backward into his head, and he gazed at Alex cruelly. The milky white pupil-less eye chilled Alex to the bone. "Give us the book. NOW."

"No," replied Alex as she pressed the book tighter.

One pirate reached out and grabbed the book, but Alex yanked it out of his hand, and the pirate screamed in agony. He withdrew a smoldering hand from the Book of Wisdom.

"Don't touch it, you dolt! The cloth! The cloth!" scolded Eyepatch as he gestured to a napkin sitting on another table. The pirates frantically scampered for the napkins, and Alex got up from the table and grabbed her loaf of bread. She briefly waved to the bartender and made her way out of the Slanted Tavern as quickly as humanly possible. The pirates chased after her, napkins in hand.

"Come back here, missy!" said Eyepatch as he chased after her through the snow with his arms outstretched. "We're humble, understanding people. Give us the book, and we will leave you alone! I give you my word!"

"I don't believe you!" yelled Alex as she ran harder and faster into the flurry of snow.

"HALT!" yelled the two men in suits as they joined the pirates' pursuit. "We said no funny business!"

The storm around them slowly turned from snow to ice as Alex departed from the village. Oh, how she wished she could have gotten supplies from that place. All she received was rejection and thieves. She ran as fast as her legs could go until the lights of the village were no longer visible, and all she could see was the flurries of snow around her. Had the pirates stopped chasing her? She'd left their village! Why would they care?

With one hand holding the Book of Wisdom and the other shielding her eyes from the storm she pressed on through the winter nightmare. Her only source of comfort was the book against her heart.

A guttural roar rattled her mind as a massive footstep thundered the ground she stood upon. Two pricks of baby blue could be seen through the storm as another thunderous footstep rattled the earth. Alex squinted through the frost and made her way boldly toward the creature. The thunderous footsteps quickened, and another roar echoed throughout the wintery wasteland. The silhouette of something large could be seen. Its shimmering blue eyes cut through the storm, glaring at her with vengeance as it advanced toward her.

Alex closed her eyes and held the book tight. "Help," she whispered. "I need help."

The cold beat her again and again as ice and snow pelted her skin. Her heart remained warm, and the book protected her, but the monster was getting closer, and she was helpless.

"I leave the ninety-nine to find the one. The good shepherd watches over you." The words echoed throughout Alex's mind.

The cold grew more bitter, but the warmth grew stronger. Keeping her alive against the perils of the winter storm. Alex stepped toward the monster. Then another. And another. Slowly advancing, it made threatening movements toward her. Gnashing its glistening teeth and glaring angrily.

"The good shepherd is with me," she whispered.

As if in response, a blinding light flooded the storm, and the pages of the Book of Wisdom glowed a vibrant white as an older man with a shepherd's staff leapt from the pages. The man was unlike anyone Alex had ever seen before, but she knew right away where he came from and that he was there to help her.

The shepherd raised his glowing staff and pointed at the monster aggressively. The monster roared in response and swung at him. The man swung his staff, and when the rod came into contact with the savage beast, it sliced its arm clean off.

The monster howled in anguish as the shepherd raised his staff and pointed at it again. It swung again, and the other arm came flying off. The shepherd raised the staff one last time, then drove it into the face of the beast, and the winds stopped. The snow froze in midair as the beast drew its last breaths before collapsing onto the snowy ground with a heavy thud. In an instant, the snow stopped pouring, and the ice quit flying. The storm stopped at once, and for the first time in history, District 2 was calm.

The shepherd smiled at Alex warmly and nodded to her as he calmly stepped back into the pages of the book, and all was silent once again. Alex, who was still in awe of what had happened, stared at the dead monster for a moment as the sounds of panicked pirates could be heard getting further and further away from her. Yelling at the top of their lungs that Alex had slayed 'the beast.'

"Hey, you."

Alex looked up, and to her surprise, the bartender from the Slanted Tavern was standing before her. He was smiling widely at her, and she gazed up at him for a second as she slowly got up from where she was.

"Who are you?" she asked, her mind briefly flashing the kissing couple she had seen in District 10, but she shook this thought out of her mind.

"You can call me Dash," he said warmly.

"Dash?"

"Yeah." He shuffled his feet and put his hands in his pockets. "I don't want to be insensitive or rude, but I haven't seen anything like this happen before in a long time. Do you have room for one more person?"

"What?"

"I want to join you. You could use a traveling companion. I mean, only if you want one, of course," replied the Dash quickly.

Alex smiled back at him and replied, "I would be delighted to travel with you."

"You would?"

"Of course," she replied. "I'm heading to District 3 next. We can go together."

Dash smiled eagerly, and together they ventured out of District 2 as the angry pirates watched from a distance. "He's a traitor," growled Eyepatch as he lowered his spyglass. "he's betrayed our town and has been sentenced to death. He's in cahoots with that rogue." He put up his spyglass again. "Luckily, they won't make it far. The pass is up ahead. We'll cut 'em off there."

Chapter Six

Spite's Pass

Alex and Dash journeyed on together through the rest of District 2, talking together as their feet sloshed through slush and melted ice.

"I can't believe I finally found another person who has a book!" he kept saying as he pulled out his own Book of Wisdom from his pocket and showed Alex excitedly.

The young woman smiled back at him and nodded as thoughts swirled in her head. She wasn't entirely certain how long Dash had been in District 2, but judging by his enthusiasm, he had been there a while.

"Where you sent here too?"

"Yup!"

"And you rode the steam train?"

"Yup!"

"And—"

This conversation carried on for a long while as Dash excitedly pelted Alex with questions. She didn't mind. He hadn't been with another soldier of the King for a long time and wanted to know everything that had happened since he left on his quest.

"And you're saying He's still trying to bring His people Home? He's still waiting for." He gasped, then whispered, "Look."

Alex looked up, and before them was a massive row of mountains spanning as far as the eye could see. Their sharp, pointed peaks could be seen reaching toward the turbulent sky above. Lightning flashed in the distance, and the two came to a halt as they gazed at the terrifying mountain pass.

"District 3," murmured Dash as he took deep breaths in and out. "We've made it to the border." He anxiously looked around the melted wasteland, which contained more water than snow.

"Let's go," said Alex boldly as she stepped forward, Dash following nervously behind.

The mountains got closer, and the light around them slowly faded to dim. The world they knew turned into a land of rock and dust. Storms and rain. They pressed on as the howling winds picked up, and water fell relentlessly onto them, soaking them to the bone. The world around them consisted of jagged, uneven surfaces that prevented them from resting or taking a moment to breathe. The further they journeyed, the more the rain weighed them down. Lightning struck the gnarled peaks, producing ominous shadows as the bolts of energy blipped down from the sky. Almost as if it were trying to intimidate t hem.

"How much further?" said Dash with a shiver as he looked around at the stormy chaos.

"I'm not sure," said Alex as she pressed on through the black. "We have to keep going. We must reach District 10 and put an end to this madness."

KAWWW.

Lightning struck, and thunder boomed as the earsplitting shriek of what could be described only as a dying croak split the stormy ambiance. A massive shadow flashed over them, and instinctively, Alex and Dash hid underneath an overhang. The jagged rocks pressed violently into their backs as a big winged something circled over them.

KAWWW KAWWW.

Lightning flashed its massive shadow cast onto the rock before them as a great clap of thunder accompanied their terror.

Black feathers scattered everywhere as a great CRASH echoed throughout the pass as the creature landed on the rocky ground.

"KAWWW. I sthay. Whath do we haveth here?"

Then they saw it. A massive crow covered in rugged black feathers with various bones caught in its knotted wings. The eyes of the bird were milky white, for it lacked pupils, and its beak had cuts and scars across it, almost as if it had clawed itself.

"KAWWW."

It roared at it and snapped its beak at Alex as it looked her up and down.

"Isn't thisth interesting," it growled as it gazed at them with its nasty, bone-colored eyes. "Theresth two of you."

"Yeah," murmured Alex as she stared at the creature and shook violently. "Now, leave us alone."

"KAWWW!" roared the bird, and Alex jumped back, pressing herself against the rocky wall. "I've never en-countered THWO exthplorers here before," it muttered as it snapped its beak at them.

"Leave us alone," said Dash nervously.

"I think not!" cackled the bird. "You thwo will make an exthellent addition to the collecthon. Another young pair to tempt."

It snapped its beak at them more ferociously as it tried to claw its way toward them. Bones swayed in its gnarled wings as it inched as close as it could to them. Alex could smell its breath, causing her to gag as she pressed herself close to the wall, clutching the Book of Wisdom for dear life.

"Justh a little bit closther," hissed the bird as it nipped its beak at them. The sharp mouth got closer and closer to Alex as it tried to bite at her violently.

Dash looked from the bird, then to Alex, then in one fluent motion, drew out his Book of Wisdom and smacked the beak with it. The bird screamed and immediately pulled out from under the overhang and let out an angry KAWWW. Lightning flashed more violently, and the bird gazed under the overlook with its milky eyes.

"You possessth purity," it hissed. It licked its beak as it gazed hungrily at Alex and Dash. "I'll be back for you."

It beat its black wings, and a couple of bones came falling to the ground as it took off with a great KAWWW and flew into the air. The sounds of its wings grew fainter and fainter as the sounds of thunder and rain overtook the world once again.

"Let's get out of here," whispered Alex and Dash nodded vigorously. They ran out of the overhang and took off through the pouring rain through the pass. Lightning flashed and thunder roared as they made their way around boulders and dead trees, past glistening lifeless fungi, and lightning until a light could be seen. Barly visible through the pouring rain and shadows around them.

"We're almost there!" yelled Alex as she shielded her eyes from the rain. Here body felt like lead as the weight of the water weighed her down, but she didn't care. They had to make it to the next district.

KAWWW.

"Oh no," moaned Dash as he looked up, shielding his eyes from the pelting rain.

"Run!" yelled Alex as they charged for the exit to the pass. The winged nightmare soaring overhead as they ran as fast their legs could go.

"Hello, sthupper, here I come." It cackled as it dive-bombed, sharp claws outstretched, ready to snatch them in its talons. Bones of its previous victims fell from its wings as it came closer and closer toward them. Alex pulled her Book of Wisdom out and held it above her head.

"PROTECT YOURSELF!" she yelled.

Dash nodded and pulled out his book, too and shielded himself as well. The exit was so close. They had to make it.

"KAWWW," roared the bird as it came down upon them, and its sharp talons grabbed the book. There was a thunderous scream and a crack of lightning as the bird was struck by an energy that didn't originate from the mountain pass. The smell of smoke and smolder could be heard, and the sounds of frantic wings growing fainter could be heard as the bird flew away as fast as it could go. Alex and Dash lowered their books, relieved to see they were not damaged, and exited the pass. Running into a market square full of bustling people.

"That was close," breathed Dash as he smiled at Alex. The two looked around as their vision swirled in and out, as they looked around blurry-eyed at the market around them.

"That was quick thinking, Alex. We almost fell into..."

"A trap."

Click.

Alex and Dash both turned, and there, standing in the crowd was 'Eyepatch' and his crew of pirates. The pirate captain had his gun drawn, and he had it aimed at them.

They had fallen right into their net.

Chapter Seven

The Market

"Hello, Alex," whispered Eyepatch as he looked Alex up and down. Alex stared at the pirate, terrified, as she stared at him in disbelief.

"How did you find us." She stared at the vile man, her eyes filled with worry and concern as the bustling townspeople strutted across the cobblestone streets.

"Tis simple," cackled Eyepatch as he smiled with his gun raised. "You are on a daring mission to stop the master from completing his superweapon. We are here to ensure you don't live to tell the tale." He raised his weapon and gave Alex a toothy smile. "Such a pretty lass, isn't that right, fellas?" He let out a vile, cruel laugh that shook the foundation of Alex's mind as he drew closer toward her with a clammy hand outstretched.

"You would make a fine worker of District 10! A fine prize for a fine ransom! I wonder how much Ash would pay for someone such as yourself?"

Dash put a hand up. "NO!" he yelled.

"HA!" roared Eyepatch as he aimed his weapon at him instead. "Don't play the hero on me, boy! We both know you don't have what it takes!"

The pirates laughed and jeered at Dash's pitiful attempts at protecting Alex, and the young woman sighed.

"It seems you only have one option, lass," said Eyepatch as he gestured for Alex to move with his gun. "Off you go."

The pirates chuckled at their captain, and together, they marched through the streets of the market, watching as the citizens continued to trade and barter. Uninterested in Alex and Dash's captivity. Alex could hear hear birds singing sorrowfully and winds blowing in a depressed, blue way. The world around them seemed hopeless despite the cheery faces within the town. Alex tried to look around at District 4 and its abundance of commerce but found nothing worth buying or doing as she continued to march with the pirates. Whatever the trap in this place was, at least they were avoiding it.

"Hello, sir!" came a friendly voice.

Alex and Dash looked up. A young man in a brown smock had approached Eyepatch and his gang.

"What do you want?" sneered Eyepatch as he glared with his good eye at the merchant.

"I want to check your license," replied the man as he reached out a hand to the pirate.

"License?" roared Eyepatch as he drew his gun and aimed it at the merchant. "And what kind of people do ye think we arrreee?" He fired two quick shots at him and the man, and two bullet holes appeared in his chest. The merchant fell backward onto the ground with a hollow thud.

"Now, if nobody else has a problem, we shall be on our way," spat Eyepatch as he reloaded his gun.

"I still want to check your license."

Everyone whirled around and watched in utter horror as the man in the brown smock slowly got up from the ground, bloodless bullet wounds and all, and turned to face the pirate as he carefully cracked his neck with his hands. The pirate's mouth hung open for a moment as he stared at the merchant, who moments before seemed harmless.

"Look, I love a good joke as much as the next guy," continued the man in the brown smock. "But you need a license to haul captives or slaves here. It's the 274th rule of trade. Now, if you don't have a license, you will be escorted out."

"But—" began Eyepatch.

"I am sorry, sir, but those are the rules," replied the man in the brown smock as he motioned for the pirate to follow him.

Eyepatch sighed, realizing that his weapons were useless here, and allowed the man in the smock to escort him out of the village along with his crew.

Alex and Dash, who couldn't believe their good fortune, excitedly ran through the rows of stalls, beckoning for buyers to come with their hard-earned money. They saw stalls for every kind of good or service imaginable. Towels and shirts, axes and merch. This place had it all.

Alex stopped at one of the stalls surrounded by mirrors, and a young woman in a pink smock greeted her. "Hello there, dear. Are you looking for the love of your life?" she asked.

Alex looked at the mirrors hanging around her and nodded vigorously.

"Excellent!" cried the woman as she clapped her hands excitedly. "It is such a wonderful thing to fall in love! Let me see. What would help you here?" She thought for a moment as she walked around in her stall, then with a little 'ah ha', she reached for a circular mirror hanging up on the wall and brought it down to the counter. "Take a look into this one, dear," she said excitedly. "I think you'll find what you're looking for. The best daydream anyone could ask for."

Alex gazed into the glassy depths, and to her surprise, a familiar silhouette of two figures holding each other formed within the glassy surface. Had she seen this before? The two lovers seemed locked in a loving kiss, and Alex slowly approached the mirror with a hand outstretched. Her eyes filled with a longing to be held and loved like that.

"That will be 35 years," said the young woman as she speedily calculated the total with an abacus.

"35 what?" asked Alex as she stared at the young woman with a frown.

"35 years," replied the woman as she smiled at Alex. "You pay with years of your life. If you want this daydream, you'll have to spend 35 years procuring it. Or you can make a one-time payment now, and we will give it to you in what feels like seconds. You won't feel a thing. All sales are final."

Alex thought about it for a moment. It was only 35 years. She could afford to lose a few of those, couldn't she? She was pretty young, after all, and the longing to be held by someone was burning strongly within her.

"Alex!"

Alex turned in time to see Dash running toward her with two merchants chasing after him from behind. The romantic mirror would have to wait.

"Get back here!" yelled one as he raised a fist into the air.

"You need to pay for that! That's 65 years!"

"Dash, what have you done!" cried Alex as she sighed and ran over to Dash. "I got you something!" said Alex proudly.

"You got me something?" asked Alex, dumbfounded as she watched the merchants grow closer and closer.

"Yep!" said Dash proudly.

"Dash, I'm sure it's nice, but you need to return it," sighed Alex as she pointed toward the merchants.

"But I thought buying financial stability would—"

"I appreciate that, Dash, but the merchant says it costs 65 years," replied Alex. "Besides, you can't pay 65 years of your life! That's too expensive!"

"For financial stability, it might be fairly priced!" exclaimed Dash as he clutched a golden dollar sign to his chest.

"Trust me, Dash. It's not, now put it back," replied Alex as she pointed at the merchants.

"That's right, kid. Put it back," demanded one of the merchants. "You can only have that if you pay for it!"

Dash sighed and, after a few moments of hesitation, handed the merchant the golden dollar sign.

"So, about that daydream offer?" asked the woman in the pink smock. "Because I like you, I'll knock five years off. That's 30 years final total."

Alex turned back to the mirror and gazed at the silhouettes holding each other. The longing returned, and she began to desire such a relationship for herself as she slowly reached out toward the mirror in desperation for this person.

"What's that?" asked Dash as he gazed curiously at the mirror.

"Nothing," said Alex hastily as she immediately stood in front of the mirror.

"Are you sure? It sounded like you were going to buy it?" asked Dash as he frowned at his friend.

"Don't be ridiculous," said Alex as she slowly began to walk away from the stall. "I was just looking."

Dash shrugged, and together, they made their way down the rows of stalls.

"Those two right there!" yelled a voice. Dash turned and began to run.

"After them! After them, I say! They attempted to burglarize my shop!" roared one of the merchants as he pointed a shaking finger at Alex and Dash.

A police whistle blew, and Alex ran after Dash. "Dash! Did you take anything else?" she yelled.

"Only a family house and a decent education!" yelled Dash as he ran as fast as his legs could go.

"Stop in the name of the law!" yelled the cops as they chased after them. "You owe 89 years to Stall #23. Get back here!"

They ran as fast as their legs could go through the confused streets of merchants and shopkeepers, jumping out of their way as they made a break for it.

"Where is the end of this market!" yelled Alex as the sounds of police whistles could be heard growing louder and louder as the cops approached faster and faster.

"I don't know!" wailed Dash. "I just wanted some stability in my future!"

"But you have to earn those things!" cried Alex as she ran out of breath through the blur of shops and stalls. "You can't just cut to the top like that!" In that moment, she remembered how hasty she had been to buy the daydream mirror and how she didn't want to work for a relationship, but she quickly shook this thought out of her mind.

"There doesn't seem to be an end to this place!" yelled Dash. "How big is District 4?"

"I don't know!" cried Alex. "It can't be much bigger!"

They continued to run further, and to their dismay, the sounds of whistles could be heard from in front and behind. They were surrounded.

"What do we do now?" yelled Alex as she tried her hardest to find another option.

Dash looked around frantically, then pointed to the ground. "There!"

Alex looked down at the cobblestone streets and saw a manhole sitting in the streets. The sewers.

"Dash, you're a genius!" she cried. She immediately ran over to the manhole and lifted the lid to reveal a slimy ladder descending into the depths of District 4. Dash immediately began climbing down the mysterious metal ladder into the depths. Alex began climbing down, too, as the merchants and officers rounded the corner. Their hands were outstretched, their legs running so fast they were a blur. Their feet not touching the ground. Little black strings could be seen attached to their arms and legs, and Alex slowly looked up, and to her horror, a giant with a black mustache and a bowler hat could be seen towering above the shopping district. Two massive puppet playboards were in his hands as he carefully controlled all of his merchant puppets to chase after Alex at ferocious speeds.

Alex grabbed the top of the manhole and immediately closed it just as the puppets reached her. There was a great CRASH of tangled strings and wooden pieces as the merchant puppets of District 4 fell into a heap, and the giant in the bowler hat faded away back into the shadows.

Plotting his next move to recapture Alex as his slave in the depths of District 10.

Chapter Eight

Frozen Labyrinth

For many moments, it was nothing about unseen rungs of a ladder and the sounds of Alex's breath. The deeper she descended into the dark, the colder the world became. After many moments of silence, the ladder came to an abrupt stop, and the sewer system was revealed. Lit by the eerie fluorescent glow of teal blue lanterns was a frozen river sitting in a massive stone tunnel stretching as far as the eye could see in both directions.

"Dash?" yelled Alex as her voice reverberated off the hard stone.

"Yes?" called a voice.

"Where are you?"

"Over here!"

Alex turned and squinted down the tunnel. She could see the faint silhouette of Dash waving to her, and she immediately ran across the frozen stone. Her shadow raced along the walls as she passed by rows and rows of mysterious lanterns and their blue flames. When Alex caught up with Dash, she stopped to catch her breath, panting as she slowly looked up at her adventuring companion.

"Look," whispered Dash.

Alex turned, and she stopped. Before her was a living room complete with a television, a tall tripod lamp, and a rug below. The unnerving part wasn't that this was covered in snow and ice. Nor was it that the couch sitting amongst it all looked brand new. It was who was sitting on it. An older man covered in icicles and snow was frozen to the couch, a mug of iced coffee in hand and a winter jacket on his person, complete with a scarf around his neck. A pair of glasses sat on the man's cold face, and he stood there, motionless, stuck to the spot he had sat down upon goodness knows how long ago.

"What happened?" breathed Alex as she looked the frozen man up and down nervously.

"I don't know," murmured Dash as he carefully looked around the couch. The tripod lamp was casting a similar eerie glow to that of the lanterns above. An ominous teal blue.

Alex peered around the man, and to her surprise, three smaller stone tunnels could be seen behind the couch. Each tunnel had a metal sign with the words 'Fear,' 'Phobia,' and 'Death,' engraved on them, respectively.

"What do you make of it?" asked Dash as he peered around to look at the tunnels and their mysterious signs.

"I don't know," replied Alex. She stepped around the couch and approached the first tunnel labeled 'Fear.' She squinted through the dark but could see nothing. "It seems we have to choose a path."

Crack.

The sounds of a neck cracking split the silence, and grinding ice could be heard. Alex whirled around to see the frozen man shift on the couch. The chunks of ice attached to his person moved with him, almost as if they were a part of his body.

He opened his mouth and breathed in for a moment, then slowly let it out.

"Welcome to District 5," he said ominously. "The entrance to the lower levels."

He cracked his neck again, causing small chunks of ice to fall off him and land on the stone ground, shattering upon impact.

"What do you want," whispered Dash as he slowly backed away.

The man turned his head all the way around to face Alex, who was standing behind him, and said in a guttural voice:

"The entrance to the lower levels,
Is colder than you know.
A decision now must be made,
To dictate where you'll go.

You could choose the path of fear,
Forever scared by all.
You could live with your worst nightmare,
High reward, greater fall.

You could choose the path of death,
And pass away abruptly,
But if you're trying to get somewhere,
It shan't be taken lightly.

Those are your choices,
I hope you choose them wisely,
For if you do not think them through,
The consequences will be costly."

There was a terrifying shriek, then the sounds of ice shifting against one another, then silence as the man turned back around and became motionless once again. Alex and Dash stared at the frozen man for many moments as if they were expecting him to do something else.

"Three options," whispered Dash as he gazed at the three tunnels.

"Yeah," murmured Alex as she looked from the man then back to the tunnels. A warmth filled her heart as the Book of Wisdom grew hot, and Alex, for the first time in a while, turned to look at its pages. "Help us to choose a path," she whispered. She opened the book, and a bright white light erupted from the pages. A stream of white shot out and flew around them like a joyous child playing outside. It flew around Dash, and he laughed joyfully as it dove under his legs and around his head. Then it flew around Alex and filled her heart with love and joy she hadn't felt in a while, reminding her of her mission to the

King. The light then circled around and flew down the Death tunnel and faded out of sight.

"What?" asked Dash as he frowned to stare at the tunnel. "Death? Why would we want to die? I thought the whole point of this was to get to District 10 to bring the King's forces in?"

"I thought so too," said Alex with a frown as she gazed down the third tunnel, which was as black as the others. "This seems very counter intuitive. Why would the King want us to die?"

They both stood there for a moment, then Alex sighed. "Alright. If the King says this is the right way, then this is the way we shall go."

"Are you mental?" asked Dash as he turned to stare at Alex.

"This is the way the book told us to go," said Alex as she shrugged her shoulders.

"Did you not hear that guy's speech?" asked Dash as he pointed to the frozen man. "He said choosing death would not be taken lightly. You know what death is, right?"

"Yeah," replied Alex as she nervously turned to face the third tunnel. "But I devoted my life to the King. If He wants me to die, then that's what I shall do."

"But—" began Dash.

"I'm not going to debate this, Dash. Right now, I have a mission to complete. Are you coming or not?"

Dash opened his mouth, then closed it.

"Come on," said Alex. She marched around the frozen couch and toward the third tunnel. Dash reluctantly followed close behind. They stepped into the tunnel; the sounds of their footsteps ricocheted off the frosted stone walls.

"See?" said Alex. They both took another step forward. SLAM.

An ice door closed behind them, and, in an instant, they were surrounded in darkness.

"AHHH!!!!" yelled Dash.

"Don't panic!" yelled Alex. "There's got to be a way out of here!"

That's when the floor beneath her gave way, and she, too, yelled as she fell down, down, down into the depths of the ground. Deeper and deeper into the black. It was an odd sensation, feeling the wind rushing around her but being unable to see anything.

The flash of a prison cell could be seen to her left as a streak of torchlight shot past on her way down. Then, there was the glistening of something big, with red eyes and sharp teeth. Its ambient growling flew past her as she continued to fall.

Alex didn't know how far she was falling but regretted her tunnel choice. The death tunnel was going to kill her! Of course it was! She continued to fall, and with a great CRASH, she landed in a pile of something.

Alex slowly opened her eyes and looked around as her body slowly overcame the shock of the fall. Whicker and straw? She wasn't sure; all she knew was she was alive, and something hay-like had broken her fall. Scratchy and itchy strands rubbed up against her skin, and she struggled to climb out for a moment. She got to her feet and collapsed out of the pile in a heap.

She got up from where she lay and looked around as her vision adjusted to the dim light. Walls could be seen all around her save for an exit off to her left. She slowly made her way over to the exit, but to her dismay, another wall greeted her just beyond that. Now, the exit had turned into a hallway to her right. She followed the wall until she came to a crossroads. One hall went left, one went forward, and one went right. A maze.

Alex sighed and looked around at the darkness around her. She tried to speak but found herself unable to. The crushing feeling of the maze felt like weights upon her vocal cords. She felt for the Book of Wisdom but couldn't find it. She immediately ran as fast as she could back to the pile of hay, but the room had vanished. In its place was another crossroads.

What was she going to do? She'd lost the book. She sighed, hung her head, and slowly began to traverse the mysterious maze. A pair of eyes watched her from above as she made her way around the labyrinth of passages. Cruelly observed her every move as she made her way through the maze with no guidance or direction.

Aimlessly walking into a trap.

Chapter Nine

Shipyard

Alex continued to walk through the dark maze. The sounds of fires crackling in the dim light could be heard as she nervously stepped around. Half expecting something to jump out at her at any moment. She took shaking breaths in and out. The air had gotten colder since the fall, or had it always been that way? The clammy hands of depression groped its skeletal hand around her heart, and she shivered as the cold flowed through her body.

Left. Right. Straight. Right. Left. Right. Right. Straight.

Her journey through the labyrinth was wearing her down. Every passageway looked the same, and she wasn't certain if she had been somewhere before or if she were somewhere new. Every wall felt like an old friend, and even the frozen fungi clutching to the sides of the icy stone gave nothing away. Alex squeezed her eyes shut, suddenly aware of how quiet it was. She had gotten so used to the whispering voices of the Book of Wisdom she had tuned them out consciously. Now that they were gone, the silence was loud.

She continued on her journey through the twisting tunnels.

Right. Straight. Straight. Straight. Left. Left. Right. Left. Straight. Left.

The confusing turns and identical-looking walls felt familiar and alien at the same time. How was she going to solve this with no help? It felt impossible.

"Help," whispered Alex as she shivered in the cold. Maybe her King would hear her?

"Hello, Alex," came a voice.

Alex turned; her eyes were full of hope, and her gaze landed on a woman with three heads. She wore the same clothes as Alex, and upon closer inspection, she realized the three heads were all on the same face: hers.

"Hello," they all said at once.

"Hi," said Alex as she looked at the three-headed Alex up and down. "Did my King send you?"

"A king sent us," they replied, and Alex shrugged. Sounded legit enough.

"Do you know which way is the way out?" asked Alex hopefully and all three heads nodded with wide smiles.

"First, you take a left," said the first head.

"Then go straight until you run into a statue," said the second.

"Then take a right," finished the third.

Alex thought for a moment. Left, straight, right. Sounded simple enough.

The three heads smiled widely as they all gazed at Alex with overenthusiasm.

"Thank you!" said Alex as she began to move as fast as she could down the left path. Sure enough, after going straight for a little while, she encountered a stone figure up ahead. She squinted at it for a moment and realized it was a statue of a man in a tweed jacket with a bowler hat. She shivered as memories of District 10 wafted through her mind like an unwelcome breeze. To think she was going back to it! But only to destroy it.

She turned right, and to her surprise, the maze opened up into a massive subterranean cove. Dark waters similar to the water Alex encountered in the first district greeted her, and, in the distance, just out of view, was a ship. Her hull was ornamented with complex carvings and fine detail work. Two sails could be seen attached to its tall mast. Alex looked around and, to her luck, spotted a couple of row boats tied to a post. She quickly untied one and got in. Rowing across the black waters toward the ship. As she got closer, the air grew musty, and the smells of rotting flesh filled the air. The sounds of happy music could be heard from the deck of the ship, and Alex saw a warm light above her. Fire.

She immediately climbed up the side of the ship and made her way onto the wooden deck. She saw silhouettes dancing around a massive bonfire in the center. She smiled, relieved to finally find sensible people and got closer to the fire.

"GOTCHA!"

Alex's blood turned to ice as rough hands grabbed her tightly and held her fast to where she was. A man with a scraggly black beard was looming over her. Alex knew those scars. When her eyes landed on the eyepatch, Alex sighed heavily.

"Gents! Look who just stumbled aboard!" cackled Eyepatch as he gripped Alex tighter. He brought his nasty face close to Alex's ear and whispered, "No book to protect you now, eh lass?"

"Get your hands off me," yelled Alex as she struggled to break free from Eyepatch's grip.

"Oh, that won't be necessary, miss," replied Eyepatch as he gave Alex a vile grin. "Lock her in the brig." He threw Alex at two other pirates, and they aggressively pulled her toward the wooden stairs descending. After a few moments of walking, they shoved Alex into a cell and slammed the iron shut.

"Enjoy your stay," spat one as they lumbered up to join the rest of the crew and their fire dancing.

Alex put her head in her hands and sighed heavily. She had been tricked. Who had the woman with three heads been? Why did she lead her here? To Eyepatch and his crew of brutes? She sighed again and slumped against the wooden wall as she thought about everything that had brought her here.

"Are you alright, Alex?"

Alex, who had learned better not to get close to strangers who knew her name, immediately pushed herself flat up against the wall. "Who is it?" she asked nervously as she put her fists up.

"It's me! Dash!" said the voice.

Alex squinted through the dim brig, and to her surprise, the young bartender sat on the opposite end of the cell, slumped up against the wall like her. He had his head resting on his hands as he sat there, bored and depressed.

"Dash!" she cried as she ran over to him, and they hugged for a moment. They sat in silence for a while as they waited for something to happen, but nothing did. The pirates continued partying, and they remained in the cell.

Alex sat down next to her friend and tried to think of an escape plan, but nothing came to mind. Without the Book, they were toast.

"I'm glad you're safe," she said as she glumly put her head in her hands.

"Same here," replied Dash as he smiled weakly at her. "They took my book. They used a cloth and managed to snatch it."

"Wait, you still had your book?" asked Alex suddenly as she sat up a little straighter.

"Yeah, but the pirates are keeping it in the captains' quarters," replied Dash. He shook his fist and sighed,

"I should have known they would come for vengeance. They never forgave me for abandoning the village."

Alex thought for a moment. They had to escape, but how?

Alex squeezed her eyes shut and, with all her might, called out to the King. She begged for an escape or some way to get out of the brig. She opened her eyes, but to her dismay, nothing changed. They were still trapped, and there was nothing she could do about it.

Dash sighed and cried. Tears trickled down his face as he hopelessly sat there in the corner. Alex didn't know what to say or do. They were stuck here, and there was nothing either of them could do.

"I'm so sorry, Alex," sobbed Dash as he wiped his swollen eyes with his hands. "It's my fault we are in this mess in the first place! If I hadn't stolen those goods in the market, we would never have been chased and forced down here."

Alex perked up for a moment, then whispered, "What did you steal again?"

"A house and education," mumbled Dash as he slumped against the wall once again. "Wouldn't do us much good in this instance."

"Education," whispered Alex. "Can I see that?"

Dash nodded and handed her a small brown sack and opened it. In an instant, Alex became aware of the cell's architecture. The geometry of its wooden beams and the locking mechanism on the door. She was aware of what was happening and realized that Dash was meant to get away with those items all along. The King's plan was working.

"I know how to escape," she whispered as she pointed to the cell door. "Those hinges have a weak point on the far left. If we strike it with enough force, it will give."

Dash turned to her, then back to the cell door. Then his eyes lit up. "We can escape."

"And grab the book," said Alex. "We may be smarter now, but that doesn't make us invincible. We need to get the Book of Wisdom back."

"That's right; it has weapons, too," whispered Dash, nodding knowingly.

Together, they got up and, after a couple of tries, kicked the hinges loose, and the door swung open. They snuck along the edge of the staircase and stealthily made their way toward the captains' quarters. While the pirates continued to dance, they cleverly jammed the lock and silently snuck into Eyepatch's study.

An ornate leather chair could be seen behind a carved wooden desk before them. A map and a compass were resting on its surface, and sitting on the far edge of the desk was a worn cloth with a book-shaped something underneath it.

"AH HA!" roared Eyepatch as a gunshot ruptured from behind them. Alex felt the bullet sail past her and embed itself into the wood.

The duo whipped around as Eyepatch reloaded his gun and aimed it at them.

"And what would ye be doing in here?" he roared. "This be me private quarters. GET OUT. BACK TO THE BRIG."

Alex and Dash backed up toward the desk. Their eyes briefly rested on the map, which showed all the routes and paths within the Realm of Districts. That would be handy to have.

"I know what ye be doing!" yelled Eyepatch as he raced across the room, and grabbed the cloth in his hands, and held it far away from Alex and Dash.

Alex grabbed the map and pocketed it right away and the pirate captain laughed.

"That be only good to you if you survive the monsters beyond!" he cackled as he fired another shot at them, causing his arm to jolt back abruptly.

Dash and Alex dove under the table as the pirate locked his gun again.

"What do we do?" mouthed Dash as he peered over the table. Eyepatch responded with two quick shots that sailed over their heads.

Alex thought for a moment. They needed the book. She thought a bit longer, then remembered the layout of the ship. The wheel was above them. She pointed up at the ceiling, then pretended to steer with a wheel and made a motion to jump. Dash nodded, and Alex silently counted with her fingers.

"What arrreee you doing?" demanded Eyepatch as he fired another shot over the table. "I know ye there! Get out!"

1.... 2.... 3....

Alex and Dash leapt onto the desk, and Eyepatch, who was taken aback, fired upward. The bullet sailed up into the ceiling, and the ship jolted suddenly as the whirring of the helm spinning out of control could be heard within the cabin. The bullet had hit its mark.

The ship was sailing in a circle as the out-of-control wheel spun like a top.

"You didn't leave the anchor down, did you?" asked Alex slyly.

"ARRRRRRR!!!!" roared Eyepatch as he fired at them again.

Frantic knocking came from the door as the pirates yelled for their captain.

"Not now, gents! I'm a wee bit preoccupied!" yelled Eyepatch as he fired his gun again.

"Captain! The ships on fire!" squealed a frantic pirate. "What do we do?"

"How did ye do such a thing?" cried Eyepatch as he lowered his gun and ran out of the cabin. Alex and Dash raced after him boldly onto the deck of the flaming ship. The momentum of the rapidly spinning vessel must've caused the bonfire to ignite the wooden decks.

"ARRRRR!" roared Eyepatch as he desperately tried to put the fire out. "ABANDON SHIP, ME HEARTIES!" He turned toward Alex and Dash and growled at them. Then, a vile smile covered his face as he raised the cloth with the Book of Wisdom over the fire.

"NO!" yelled Alex as she ran toward Eyepatch. The pirate raised his gun and yelled, "IT BE THE END OF THE LINE, LASS! GIVE UP, OR I'LL DESTROY YE PRECIOUS BOOK!"

Dash stood there for a moment, frozen and horrified as they thought about Eyepatch's threat.

"YE RUNNING OUT OF TIME!" yelled Eyepatch. "SURRENDER NOW."

The fire grew wilder and untamed as it licked the sides of the ship. Devouring everything it got close to.

"No! We will not give up!" yelled Alex. "We are going to destroy you and all of the districts if it's the last thing we do!"

"THEN YE ON YOUR OWN!" screamed Eyepatch as he threw the book into the fire. Alex watched almost as if it were in slow motion as the book flew into the air and landed into the flaming mass below. Eyepatch cackled at Alex and Dash's horror-struck faces as he pointed at them with a look of vile elation that didn't deserve to exist.

BOOM.

There was a thunderous explosion as the orange flames turned bright white, and the fires swirled like a massive storm.

Eyepatch turned as the pillar of white flames swirled like a tornado above them and yelled, making a break for the black waters below. A pair of white eyes could be seen through the turbulence, watching the pirate make his getaway. Then, a massive fiery arm reached out of the vortex, grabbing Eyepatch firmly and raising the evil man into the air as the white flames consumed his body causing him to burn. He yelled as he slowly turned to dust and ash.

The flaming tornado then reached out and grabbed the rest of his crew. One by one, destroying them from the inside as they tried to escape their judgement. Alex and Dash only watched in awe as the ship spun faster and faster, and the flames grew stronger and stronger. The entire ship was now ablaze in a brilliant white fire, and with power unfathomable, it rocketed them forward through the cove and into a water-filled tunnel at a speed they couldn't comprehend. As they raced across the waters, Alex ran up to the helm and grabbed the wheel. Steering them through twisting and turning tunnels. Dash manned the sails, watching from the mast as they sailed faster and faster with the help of the King.

There was another great BOOM, the ship stopped, and the white flames were sucked back into the Book of Wisdom, which lay on the deck of the mended ship, looking just as good as it had before. Not a scratch was left upon its leather surface.

"Where are we?" asked Dash as he picked up the book.

Alex pulled out Eyepatch's map and smiled to herself. "We just entered District 8."

Chapter Ten

Echoes

Alex and Dash looked around at the clearing before them. They'd skipped District 7! Alex carefully steered the vessel around one last corner, and the world opened up to another massive cavern. The ship bumped gently up against the shore, and the duo leapt out and onto the rocky surface below. Dash smiled at Alex and held up the Book of Wisdom, and together, they ventured into the cavern in search of the next threat they would encounter. On and on they went through the cavern, but all they found were stones and sticks scattered across the cold ground. The atmosphere was surprisingly charming, but Alex figured that was because of the Book of Wisdom.

"Is there supposed to be something here?" asked Dash as he looked around curiously.

"You tell me."

Alex and Dash looked up, and there, standing in front of them, was the man with the mustache and bowler hat. He twirled his stache as he looked at the two adventurers and Alex stared down the vile man. They would stop him and put an end to his whole operation.

"I don't understand you people," he said as he slowly approached them. "You are always medaling with my plans. You have acquired a reputation for being a nuisance."

"And we will continue to be a nuisance!" said Dash proudly as he held the book against his chest.

"Oh please!" said the man coldly. "You have entered what some like to call 'the front door'. I commend you for that. Now is the time for you to turn around. Take your ship back to where you came from and leave."

"Do you really think that's going to scare us?" said Alex.

"Perhaps," said the man. "You are not doing anything that concerns me. Just know you are officially stepping into my personal kingdom. From this point forth, you are not just bothering; you are trespassing. And you know what I do to trespassers." He turned to Alex and whispered, "Remember John?"

Immediately, the memories of District 10 swirled in Alex's mind as the horrifying sight of John being punched off the ledge looped again and again.

"This doesn't have to be your future," whispered the man as he twirled his mustache. "This isn't your fight. You can return to where you came from unscathed. All I ask is you take that foul book with you."

"No, this is our fight," insisted Dash, and Alex shook District 10 out of her mind.

"Yeah. We are going to destroy you," she said boldly. "We are taking back what you stole from the King."

"Then you have made your decision, I take it?" snarled the man as he clenched his knuckles to the point of joints popping.

Alex and Dash looked at each other, and the man shook with fury. "I will remember this!" he yelled as he pointed a finger at them. "You violated my kindness! You violated my hospitality!"

"You don't possess kindness," replied Alex.

"Yeah, and what hospitality?" added Dash.

"You of all people ask ME what kind of hospitality?" roared the man as he pointed at Dash. "Would you care to tell us all how you got trapped in District 2? How you ran away?"

Alex stopped and turned to Dash; her eyes filled with surprise.

"What?" she whispered.

"Oh. He didn't tell you," whispered the man as he twirled his mustache with a broad, vile smile. "Mr. Dash is one of the biggest cowards I've ever met. He ran away from his quest, gave up on his mission, and was retreating when pirates trapped him." He put his hands behind his back as he slowly circled them in the cavern. "Unable to escape, he lied to them and told them he worked as a bartender at the local tavern, and he took residence there. Forcing himself to live a lie that was never his true self."

The man vanished and reappeared next to Dash, his quivering hands grasping the Book of Wisdom tightly as the man twirled his mustache over him. "You've lived in my hospitality for quite a while, Dash. Do you care to share?" Dash slowly backed away as he gazed up, horrified at the man baring down upon him. "I'll take that as a no," replied the man as he straightened his bowler hat.

He glared at Alex and said, "I'll give you two hours to leave this place. If you do not, I will not be as courteous."

There was a flash of firelight, and the man vanished.

Dash stood there, motionless, his mouth hung open slightly as he stared at where the man had been moments before.

"Dash?" whispered Alex as she turned to her friend.

"I'm sorry," said Dash as tears trickled down his face. "I.. I..."

"It's going to be okay," said Alex as she reached out a hand.

"No! It's not okay!" cried Dash shrilly as he pulled away from her. "We're still on the Death Path, remember? The path that we chose in that frozen sewer. He's going to kill us! I know it!"

"Dash, calm down. Don't allow what he said to define who you are," said Alex as she rested a hand on Dash's shoulder.

THUMP.

The sounds of a massive footstep echoed throughout the cavern, causing the ground to rumble.

"What was that?" whispered Alex.

"Th... thhh... this is where I turned around," whispered Dash nervously as he shook all over.

THUMP.

"So, you've been here before," murmured Alex.

"Well, I snuck past the pirates and manually rowed down the tunnel," whispered Dash as he stared off as if he were reliving the moment. "It was dark and cold, then fire. Bright and angry fire."

"Like on the ship?" asked Alex, but Dash shook his head.

"What do you mean, 'fire?' Where did it come from?" asked Alex.

THUMP. THUMP. THUMP.

A massive guttural roar split the silence. A bright orange light filled the darkness, washing everything in an angry orange-red light.

"Dash, you've got to work with me here," said Alex as she looked up at the bright, fiery light. "What do you remember? Your memory may help us with what we're about to face."

Dash shook his head and whispered, "It's too difficult."

"Nothing is impossible. We have the King on our side and the Book of Wisdom in our possession," replied Alex as she gave him a reassuring pat on the back.

THUMP.

The fiery light and the roar faded to darkness and silence.

THUMP. THUMP. THUMP. THUMP.

The footsteps were getting quicker.

"It's a…" said Dash as he gasped for air. "We should go. It's going to eat us."

"No, Dash. What is it? Is it a—?"

"Bear."

The guttural roar returned, and Alex looked up to see a massive grizzly bear covered in flames. Its glowing scarlet eyes glared down upon them as its massive jaw let out a repulsive roar that caused its flames to grow bigger and angrier.

THUMP.THUMP.THUMP.THUMP.THUMP.TH UMP.

It was practically bounding toward them now as it stopped roaring, and the flames died down, making it almost invisible in the darkness of the cavern. All that could be seen were its two scarlet eyes fixated on the adventurers. Its hatred for life gave it an aura that smelled of smoke and destruction.

It let out another roar, and the flames grew bigger and angrier than before. It leapt into the air, raising a massive, clawed paw as it came down upon them.

"LOOK OUT!" yelled Alex as she grabbed Dash's hand and pulled him out of harm's way just in time.

CRASH.

The bear landed on the ground, and it roared again, causing the flames to spike higher than they thought possible. Bounding toward them as fast as its legs could go. Swinging at them with all its might to put them out of commission.

"There's got to be a way to stop this thing," yelled Alex as she ran around the cavern with Dash close behind.

"There isn't a way to stop it!" yelled Dash as he closed his eyes and covered his ears. "It's too strong."

"I don't believe that, Dash. What can we use against it? There's got to be something!" She glanced at the Book of Wisdom. "There's got to be something in here that can help us."

She paged through the different sections as fast as she could. "That's about destroying idols, that's about peacemaking," She murmured as she desperately tried to find something that would help them, for she had never actually paged through the book before. Things had just worked out in the past.

She found the part about the Shepard. That's it! In an instant, the Shepard she had met in District 2 reappeared. Instead of attacking the bear, he turned to Alex, held up his staff, and then stepped back into the book.

"That didn't work?" cried Dash. "But that guy was so powerful!" He grabbed the book and paged through it as fast as he could.

The bear roared again and leapt into the air, forcing them to relocate again.

"We need something to attack or kill it," said Alex desperately as she paged through the book quickly. "There doesn't seem to be anything about that in here."

The bear leapt into the air again. "I'm sorry, Alex. It seems like we are going to die," said Dash as he sighed sadly. He hung his head and handed her the book.

Alex thought for a moment, then her face lit up. "Wait a minute."

She watched as the bear leapt into the air again, preparing to smash them into the ground with its hatred and malice.

"We aren't supposed to do anything."

She raised the Book of Wisdom into the air and said, "I'm not going to fight you."

Ding, Ding, Ding, Ding, Ding.

Alex smiled widely as the bear fell faster and faster toward them as the faint sounds of a ringing railroad gate alarm ringing could be heard, and just as the bear was about to land on them. A loud train whistle cut through the room, and a white light blasted through the massive bear as the Joyous Express burst through its chest, and laughter filled the air as the sounds of the conductor and engineer could be heard overhead.

"He was bear-ly holding on!" said the conductor joyfully as the train came to a halt on the stone ground.

"Laughter and humor! That's the ticket!" said the engineer as he leaned on his shovel for support. "Best way to rid angry bears any day!"

They both turned to Alex and Dash, and they beamed at them.

"Were you feeling a little blue?" asked the conductor with a grin as he held up some cheese.

"Not another cheese pun!" said the engineer as he leaned on the brake lever for support.

The conductor bit into a pear and smiled childishly, then announced, "All passengers, fasten your seatbelts and look away from the windows; we are currently within the Realm of Districts. The victory is coming soon!"

There was a faint cheer from within the passenger cars, and the conductor grinned at Alex and Dash, then turned to the bear as its flames died out and it collapsed onto the ground with a heavy thud.

"I think that's the first joyful thought it had in its life," murmured Dash as he stared at the glowing white hole in its chest.

"Unfortunately, so," replied the engineer as he smiled at them warmly. "Right to the heart, too. It's a shame that it allowed anger to fester within. It gives the illusion of power and might when there really isn't any."

"The real power comes from the King," added the conductor as he took another bite into his pear. He looked at Alex and Dash. "Well? Are you ready?"

"For what?" asked Alex.

"Well, this is District 8. Just this room. It's the smallest because evil wasn't expecting anyone to defeat that bear. Beyond this are Districts 9 and 10. District 9 is more of a wall full of patrols protecting District 10 from attacks and breaches." He smiled at Alex and Dash. "You're nearly there!"

He reached out a hand for the Book of Wisdom and asked, "If I may?"

Dash eagerly handed the book to the conductor, and the man opened the book and, from within its pages, pulled out a shimmering sword.

Alex and Dash gasped in awe as the conductor handed it to them. Then, another sword was pulled out. One for each other them.

"I thought there was more in here," mumbled the conductor. "One second." He reached into the book so far that he was shoulder-deep in its pages. "Hmmm." He tipped the book upside down and shook it, and two sets of armor fell out. "There we go!" he said with a smile as he handed the sets to them.

He stepped back to admire Alex and Dash with their new armor and swords. "May the King protect you and be gracious to you," he said. "You've got this."

He gestured for them to go, and Alex frowned. "Aren't you coming with?"

"We're going to rally the troops of Kingdom," said the engineer. "Rest assured, you will not be fighting alone. You've already busted a sizeable hole in here. Once you break District 9's defenses, District 10 is vulnerable and exposed. Then it's just a matter of recapturing it."

Alex and Dash nodded, and the conductor smiled as he boarded the train. "Don't worry, my friends! We'll be back!" he called as the Joyous Express rose into the air. "Go kick evil in the pants and remind them we'll never leave it provolone!"

The sounds of laughter could be heard from the engineer as he commented on the conductor's cheese puns, and, in a heartbeat, they were gone.

Alex and Dash turned toward a passageway off to one side.

"So that was District 8," murmured Alex.

"Two more left," said Dash as he nervously looked around. "Perhaps we should wait. Then—"

"We have to break through District 9, remember?"

"Right."

They stood there in silence for a moment, then Alex whispered, "Let's go."

And without another word, they set out beyond the cavern into the next room.

They would destroy the Realm of Districts, and nothing would stop them.

Chapter Eleven

Psychological Warfare

Alex and Dash were greeted by darkness on the other side of the cavern. Their armor clinked gently against their skin as they marched forward toward District 9. Alex held up her sword, alert to anything that approached them, while Dash held the Book of Wisdom.

"Oh, hello there!"

The duo whipped around, and there, standing before them, was a woman who wore black armor across her chest, heavy leather boots, and three heads attached to her neck. Alex's clone was back.

The three heads smiled cheerfully at them as they swayed slightly.

"What do you want?" asked Alex as she raised her sword.

"No need for alarm! We're on your side!" they replied.

"You led me to a ship full of pirates," replied Alex.

"We led you out of the maze," corrected the heads. "That's all you asked of us. You can't blame us for what was waiting at the end of it."

Alex thought for a moment, then slowly lowered the sword.

"And besides," continued the first head. "We are you. Here to assist you whenever you're in peril."

"The King sent you?" asked Dash suspiciously.

"A king sent us, yes," replied the second head.

"Huh," said Alex as she stared at the three-headed woman with a frown. She sheathed her blade, but Dash didn't lower the book.

"Your friend is very untrusting," commented the third head as she smiled widely at Dash. "Why do you dislike us?"

"There's something very wrong about you," said Dash as he continued to hold up the Book of Wisdom. "I don't know what, but I do know you won't touch us as long as we have the book. That's why you're being so nice."

"Oh nonsense!" said the first head, and the other two followed suit. "We merely wanted to help you into District 9!"

"Help?" asked Alex with her eyebrows raised.

"Exactly! We'll help you get past the defenses to enable you to gain access to District 10!"

Dash and Alex looked at each other for a moment. The offer seemed possible, especially because they didn't know where they were going.

"I'm alright with that," said Alex with a shrug. She was talking to herself times three.

"Fine. But I'm watching you," muttered Dash as he slowly lowered the book.

"Splendid!" exclaimed the second head. "Follow us!" She gestured for them to follow, and together, they marched into the darkness. Creeping along the edge of rocky faces and into shadow. Alex thought she saw eyes watching them through the black, but to her relief, none of them dared get any closer.

Torchlight flashed past them, and the smell of sulfur burned in their faces. A harsh volcanic aroma that grew stronger by the second. The temperature quickly rose from chilling to sweltering as they grew closer and closer to District 9.

They walked for a time until they came to a massive black silhouette of a wall towering over them. The wall was so tall they couldn't see the top of it, and an ominous firelight illuminated its base from the depths of a moat surrounding its perimeter.

The three-headed Alex produced a metal rod from inside her armor and struck it into the ground. The sounds of grinding gears and machinery could be heard as a mechanical metal drawbridge lowered over the moat, allowing them safe passage across the flickering chasm. The woman marched on, Alex and Dash nervously following close behind. Alex peered over the edge of the drawbridge and was greeted by a face full of the sulfur smell as her eyes burned. Oozing hot lava was licking the sides of the chasm below, and Alex was suddenly very grateful they had an escort and they didn't have to try to break in themselves.

They continued into the fortified metal wall and turned a corner. Monsters covered in black armor could be seen marching around various sections of the wall. Thanks to their guide, however, they stayed hidden from the patrols. They climbed up flights of stairs past sleep-ing giants and beyond skeletal creatures with crossbow mounts. The deeper that got into the defenses, the more sophisticated the technology became. Cannons replaced crossbows; then guns replaced those. Soon enough, Alex wasn't certain what period she had stepped into. The weapons were getting progressively more powerful the deeper they went into District 9, and it became undoubt-edly clear to her they were at evil's front door.

Deeper still, they continued into the depths of District 9. The sounds of hollow laughter could be heard through the walls as the sounds of slaves of District 10 slowly came into earshot. They were almost there! Whispers from various creatures could be heard as they went:

"Yes, that's what I heard. Serenity Station, that's the plan."

"Yes. The weapon is almost armed."

"Countdown begins soon."

A weapon? Serenity Station? What did it mean? Alex thought for a while as they continued to march through the wall. The sounds of the slaves got louder and louder.

"Just one more left," chorused the three-headed Alex as the two adventurers were brought back to reality.

They stepped over piles of bones and snuck around more guards and patrols.

Within moments, they found themselves in a massive, gated entryway with a feeble man lying against a wall, fast asleep. The man seemed to be hundreds of years old and had evidently fallen asleep on the job.

"Clerk!" barked their guide, and the man woke up with a start, gazing up blurry-eyed at them all.

Clerk looked around, then mumbled, "Yes?"

"We wish to pass through," commanded the second head.

"Indeed!" chorused the first and third.

"But, I thought you said when the rocket was finished, we—"

"That's an order," said the woman stiffly.

The man sighed, slowly got up from his chair, hobbled over to a massive wheel, and began to turn it slowly, raising the gate.

"I've got places to be," said the three-headed Alex as she crossed her arms. "FASTER."

"Yes, ma'am," croaked the man as he hurriedly turned the wheel.

Within moments, they were past the gate, and together, they journeyed down another passageway lined with guards, who, to their surprise, seemed oblivious to them.

"Here we are!" announced the three-headed Alex as they stepped onto a massive overlook. "Welcome to District 10!"

Flying cars zoomed past them, and the sounds of wild laughter could be heard down below as the slaves of the Realm of Districts continued to march around doing their jobs. Unaware of the abuse they were going through physically and psychologically.

"I can't believe it," whispered Alex. She turned around to face their guide. "I can't thank you enough. You're not going to get in trouble for helping us, will you?"

The three heads looked at each other, then smiled widely. "Of course not!" they replied with a shrug.

Alex and Dash gazed over the edge of the overlook, almost leaning over as they gazed at the futuristic technology within the final District. It was almost surreal how much had changed between Districts 8 and 10. From primitive to advanced. Despite this being the literal nest of evil, Alex couldn't help but feel impressed by how advanced the capital was.

"So, what's the plan now?" asked Dash anxiously as he turned around to face their guide once again. "Do we—"

No response.

Alex frowned. "Yeah, what now—" She turned just in time to see a massive hand come around and force the mask of a sleeping apparatus onto her face. The world slurred and slowly faded into a watercolor mess of abstract. She drifted into a forced REM sleep where she dreamed about her allegiance to District 10 and her desire to work until she collapsed.

Chapter Twelve

Normalcy

Alex awoke in her dorm like she always had. Time to work. She stepped out of the dorms, brushing past housekeepers as she went as she followed her fellow workers through a subterranean walkway covered in grates. Steam hissed, and fires roared as the young woman marched on, tapping her hand against the guard rails as she went. There was something alien yet familiar about these rails. It was almost as if she had done this before. What was she thinking? She'd always done this.

"Hey, Alex! How's it going today?" asked Fred as he smiled widely and patted Alex on the back. His arm was covered in dry blood, and his neck had multiple gashes in it.

Alex smiled back and said, "Going great, Fred!"

"Check this out!" said Fred excitedly as he pointed to his neck and laughed. "I got hit by one of the saws! Isn't that hilarious?"

Alex nodded enthusiastically.

"Well, I've got to go mine some iron ore for the next fifteen hours! Wish me luck!"

Alex waved goodbye as Fred walked off down the hall, smiling and laughing.

Nobody seemed disturbed by the nasty wounds the workers had all over their persons. Alex didn't seem disturbed by it either. Her past adventures were forgotten. Everyone was smiling like before and Alex was none the wiser.

"All workers, please be sure to clock in with your worker ID before proceeding through the terminal," said a robotic voice over the intercom.

Alex nodded with a smile and swiped her red worker card into a reader, and the doors opened letting her pass through into the mining room. Metal shafts and gears turned aggressively, causing deafening clacking sounds to echo throughout the metal room. The young woman turned, and there, standing before her, was a man in a bowler hat, twirling his mustache as he watched her approach.

"What is my task, sir?" she asked, and the man's smile grew wider. Almost as if he knew something she didn't.

"Today, you shall be shoveling fuel," replied the man with a cruel smile. "Just like you always have."

Alex saluted the man, picked up a shovel, and began to shovel coal into the furnaces. Hour after hour after hour, she shoveled. Continuing the labor-intensive cycle of shovel, lift, drop. Shovel, lift, drop. Shovel, lift, drop. Her arms begged her to stop, but she didn't listen. They always did that.

This process went on for a long while as she continued to her grueling work. Shovel, lift, drop. Shovel, lift, drop.

She didn't notice that her armor had vanished. Nor that her sword was no longer present. She didn't think about where Dash could be or that they had a mission to destroy the place she was now working for. She simply continued her cycle of shovel, lift, drop. Shovel, lift, drop. Shovel, lift, drop. This carried on for a long time as she continued her work, and when she was done for the day, she left the building and made her way back to her dorm.

"All workers, please be sure to clock out with your worker ID before proceeding through the terminal to your dorms," said the robotic intercom.

Alex swiped her card and continued on her way, skipping and smiling unnaturally wide as she made her way through the subterranean tunnel once again. Up a flight of stairs and into her dorm. She lay on her bed and grabbed her sleeping apparatus.

"NO!"

A hand reached out from under the bed and grabbed the mask.

"Hey," complained Alex as she tried to rip the mask out of the firm grip of the hand, but the hand did not relent. "I need to sleep."

"Not with this junk, you won't," snapped the voice. "Come on, Alex. We have to get out of here."

"Let me sleep."

"Alex, don't allow them to poison your mind," said the voice as Dash crawled out from under the bed without letting go of the mask. In his other hand, he held the Book of Wisdom, and he brought it closer and closer to Alex's heart. "Come on, come on," he muttered as Alex fought him to bring the book any closer.

Alex's muscles were screaming at her as the two adventurers fought each other.

"I knew something was up as soon as we began following that creepy lady," said Dash as he slowly brought the book closer and closer to Alex. "I didn't put my guard down, and when she tried to stuff one of these things on me, I hit her with the book and ran away. You can call me a coward, but I knew deep down I could come back to rescue you."

Alex's eyes flashed for a moment. Her hand gave as the spell of District 10 waivered for a second. Dash brought the book down, and Alex gasped. Waking up for the first time for who knew how long.

"Dash?" she whispered.

"Yeah, it's me," whispered Dash as he smiled joyfully at Alex, and the young woman gave a smile that wasn't eerie or fake but filled with life and love. Dash helped her to her feet and sighed a sigh of relief. "I was so worried there," he said. "We've done our mission. It's time to go signal the troops of Kingdom."

"We'll have to be careful," added Alex. "I know what happened to the last person who tried to escape this place, and it wasn't pretty."

Dash nodded, and together, they stealthily made their way down the hall of the dorms, hiding the Book of Wisdom under Dash's shift as they went.

"Where is my sword and armor?" muttered Alex as they pretended to be bewitched. Nodding to housekeepers as they went to not arouse suspicion.

"I followed you after you were put to sleep to that tower over there," murmured Dash as he gestured to a watchtower covered in circuit boards and flickering lights. "From there, the defenses were too strong. I couldn't get past the guards undetected. I know when you were brought out of there, you were missing your armor, so it's probably still up there."

"Do you still have yours?" whispered Alex.

"Never took it off," replied Dash proudly. "It's hidden under my shirt."

They stepped out onto the busy streets of District 10. Making their way past smiling workers on their way to and from their grueling tasks. It was honestly sad, watching as these people obliviously ran their bodies into the ground because of their brainwashed state.

Sneaking through the crowd they made their way over toward the tower. Unfortunately, two firm guards stood at the entrance of the massive technological structure.

"Hi," said Alex as she approached the guards with the most exaggerated smile she could muster.

"Hello!" said one of the guards with a wide, empty smile. "State your business."

"We are here to grab equipment for the master," said Alex wildly.

"And what equipment is that?" asked one of the guards, who abruptly cocked her head to one side. Her smile grew unnaturally wide. They were on to them.

"I think you should go back to bed," said the other guard as he reached a hand out toward Dash.

SHINK.

In one fluent motion, Dash drew his sword and drove it through the guard, causing her to collapse onto the ground and turn to ash.

The other guard gasped, and his smile vanished, replaced instead with a vile expression of boundless cruelty.

"That is a contraband item," he growled. "Hand it over, or I will destroy you. You are not permitted to interfere with the plan!"

"You want it?" asked Dash slyly as he glanced at Alex.

"Yes, now hand it over," demanded the guard.

"Here you go," replied Dash with a shrug as he handed the sword to the guard. After touching his skin, the sword melted the guard's hand like wet paint.

"ARGGEEE!" wailed the guard as he turned to black mush and collapsed onto the ground.

Dash picked up the weapon, smiled and turned to Alex. "I think he forgot to use a cloth." Alex laughed.

Together, they ran up a flight of glowing red stairs. Electric lights lined the edges of their foreboding, sleek architecture.

"Okay. We're going to grab your armor and sword, and then we can signal the army," said Dash as he turned to Alex, who nodded enthusiastically.

"Do you think anybody is up here?" asked Alex as they continued to ascend the spiraling red staircase.

"Probably," replied Dash. "We'll have to find out."

No further adversaries appeared for the rest of the climb upward. When they reached the top, they spotted the armor and sword sitting in the center of the room. Sitting eerily on a table of blackened wood.

"That was easier than I expected," admitted Alex as she ran over to the table.

"I know. I thought for sure they would station a couple of guards up here at the very least," said Dash as he held up his sword, checking the empty room for threats. "I guess they were so confident in how brainwashed everyone is they didn't bother."

Alex put on her armor and fitted her sword into its sheath.

"You ready?" asked Dash as he smiled warmly at her.

"I'm ready."

"Let's go wreck this place," said Dash excitedly. They raced for the stairs but stopped in their tracks. The stairs had vanished. The floor was one long sheet of blackened wood, and the hole they had come up through was no longer there.

"Where are the stairs?" asked Dash with a frown.

"They were right here," whispered Alex as she ran over to where the stairwell had been moments before. "Where did it go?"

"That's a good question, Alex. Where DID the stairs go?" whispered a voice.

Alex and Dash slowly turned, and there, towering over them, was the three-headed woman. Their guide had led them into a trap.

Her arms were outstretched, and the two adventurers raised their swords. The three heads gnashed their teeth as they all glared down upon them.

"Why are you in here?" they roared as they all growled at Alex.

"We're here to destroy this place," replied Alex.

"HA!" said the woman as she glared at them. "As the Head of Security, I cannot allow that. If you intend to sabotage my rocket, you'll have to go through me."

Alex and Dash looked at each other briefly in confusion. Rocket? There was never a mention of a rocket. Then Alex's memory jolted, and she remembered whispers from the guards of District 9. How Clerk had mentioned something about a rocket. What did it mean?

"Yes, we are here to disable your rocket," said Alex as she raised her sword at the Head of Security. "And it will never get anywhere as long as we're here to stop you."

A smile curled across the three heads as they all began not to chuckle at Alex and Dash.

"You don't know, do you?"

Alex and Dash looked at each other, then back at the three-headed woman.

"Do you seriously think we just enslave people and call it a day?" She laughed maniacally, and the tower shook as if it were trembling in fear. "Our workers have been forging metals and building up our defenses since day one. You really think we didn't know this day would come? When your little Kingdom attempts to reclaim the land WE own?" She chuckled, and her eyes sparkled with an empty void that could never be filled. "Little do you know. Oh yes, little do you know. The reason for the mining operation in the first place."

"Tell us what you're up to," demanded Alex as she stepped forward and drew her sword.

"No," replied the Head of Security as she began to chuckle again. "Just like all the shadows who reside here, I prefer to leave you in the dark. And that is exactly what I'm going to do." She raised her fists and punched Alex backward, causing her to fly across the room and slam into the wall. The Head of Security shook her fist for a moment as if she had been burnt, but then advanced toward Dash. The young man swung at her with his sword, but the woman was too quick. She kicked him in the legs, and he, too, was thrown backward into the wall. Both were weakened from the sudden blows.

The three-headed monster of a woman raised her arms, and held up two sleeping apparatuses and advanced toward them. "This time, there will be no mistake," she growled as she loomed closer toward them.

It was at this moment a trumpet fanfare sounded throughout the world of District 10. Royal and regal were the notes as the walls of District 9 rumbled.

The Head of Security immediately turned toward the sound of the rumbling and then clicked her fingers. The stairwell reappeared, and she immediately ran down it, resealing the floor after she left.

Alex turned to Dash weakly as they lay against the tower wall and slowly smiled at him.

The army of Kingdom had come.

Chapter Thirteen

Shadows Play

Alex and Dash sat there in silence as the sounds of rumbling thundered throughout District 10. Too weak to stand. Her ribs were screaming at her as she tried to get up.

"We're trapped in here," moaned Dash as he looked around at the tower room. "How are we supposed to help Kingdom if we're trapped in here?"

"I don't know," said Alex as she tried with all her might to get back up again.

Another rumble shook the foundation of the wretched land as District 9 was pummeled yet again by the forces of Kingdom.

"Look at the bright side, the King is coming to rescue us."

They smiled at each other as they tried to move.

"We did it," croaked Dash as he slowly put a fist into the air.

"Yeah," whispered Alex as she clutched her side as the pain continued to radiate throughout her chest.

Tap. Tap. Tap.

"What was that?" asked Dash as he looked around wildly.

"I'm not sure," said Alex as she slowly looked up toward the ceiling. "Something's trying to get in."

KAWWW.

In an instant, a massive black something burst through the ceiling, and to their horror, the massive, winged nightmare landed on the black floor. Shaking a couple of bones out of its feathers, the crow scanned the room with its milky white eyes and scarred beak and cackled softly.

"What do we havth here?" it leered as it looked Alex and Dash up and down.

"Thwo little adventherers stuck in a tower."

It opened its beak and turned to Alex. "No purity in sight."

It turned to Dash. "Perfecthly vulnerable."

It opened its mouth, let out a KAWWW and laughed. "Fresh meat." It bolted toward Alex, and she desperately shifted as fast as she could as the massive crow slammed its beak into the wooden wall, missing her by inches. The young woman felt too fatigued to fight back. The bird turned its eerie pupil-less eyes toward her, let out another KAWWW and proceeded to slam its beak at her again.

"Stop," groaned Dash as he weakly got up and tried to grab the crow and pull it away from Alex. The monster only shook him off and continued to assault Alex, its attempts getting closer and closer as the young woman slowly ran out of energy.

Alex's mind slowly faded to a swirling mist. Two silhouettes kissing each other. How she longed to be just like them. She reached out toward them, letting the false scene take control of her mind. The mist became denser as she tried to see who was holding the woman. Desperately wafting the atmosphere out of the way. She longed to know who her lover was.

The silhouette of the man turned to her and stopped embracing the young woman as Alex approached. "Hello, Alex," said the man as he looked at her with his unseen eyes.

"Hi," said Alex excitedly.

"Do you want to be with me?" asked the man as he reached out a hand for Alex to hold.

Alex nodded enthusiastically. No more being alone. She now felt loved and cared for. Her desire took over her mind as the mist became denser still, and the man got closer and closer.

When her eyes adjusted to the light, her mouth fell open. The silhouette was Dash. Alex stepped back for a moment, then whispered, "That can't be right."

"Why can't it be right?" asked Dash as he advanced toward her.

"No, this is wrong. I can't be with you," she said as she stepped back.

"But you desire it deep down," said the Dash silhouette. "You've wanted this since day one. Why hold back?"

"I—" began Alex, but she hesitated. Temptation seeping into her mind as the shadowy Dash grew closer to her, the silhouette of the woman fading from sight.

"Be with me," whispered Dash as he reached a shadowy hand out for Alex to hold.

Alex began reaching out toward him. Withdrawing her hand a few times as she thought about it. Would it be wrong? There was nobody telling her not to.

A scream echoed throughout the misty landscape as the female silhouette put her hands up and ran toward the shadowy Dash.

"Honey, dear! He's coming to slay us!" she cried.

"Not now, darling," grunted the shadow Dash.

"But dear! He's right—"

In an instant, the shadowy woman collapsed onto the ground as she fainted from the stress.

"OY! Freako!"

The shadowy Dash whirled around, and there, standing in the mist, was Dash. He had his sword drawn and was pointing it at the shadowy imposter.

"Oh, this will be good," snarled the shadow as he approached Dash and drew a black sword. "What do you want, boy? You are interrupting a perfectly good fantasy."

"There is nothing good about what you're doing!" yelled Dash as he raised his sword. "Stay away from my friend!"

"Oh really?" snapped the shadow as he drifted toward the young warrior. "And why would you care? You struggle with the same temptation, too, you know. Why not indulge yourself in the world your heart desires?"

In an instant, the silhouette of the woman got back up, and Alex realized for the first time that the shadow woman looked like her. It made sense now.

"I'm not going to allow you to control my life any longer!" replied Dash as he began to approach the shadows. "You are not the boss of me or my life."

"But you cannot deny you like her," cackled the shadow as he drifted around the misty world. "You romanticize about Alex all the time, longing to be with her."

"I've changed," said Dash boldly as he held up his sword firmly.

"OH REALLY?" screamed the shadow as he advanced closer and closer toward Dash. "And what have you changed about yourself? Nothing! You are still the pathetic, easily persuaded child who acts upon impulse. Running away when life gets hard. Falling for the simplest tricks. You will never be anything more than who you are. It's a fact."

The shadow cackled more with gnarly dark arms outstretched. "You haven't changed at all."

Dash looked at his doppelganger straight in the eyes, then said, "You've forgotten one very important thing."

"And WHAT is that?' snarled the shadow.

"I no longer think about her in that way," replied Dash with a shrug.

The shadow laughed and pointed a finger at the young man. "Your romantic daydreams haven't changed! You are still as weak as you were before."

Dash smiled at the shadow, then said, "I'm patient now."

"What?" snapped the shadow in surprise. "No, you're not—"

"I'm also kind," said Dash as he stepped forward.

"You can't say that—" began the shadow.

"I do not envy, I do not boast. I'm no longer proud."

The shadow began to back away quicker toward Alex as he made a hasty retreat away from the advancing Dash.

"I shall not dishonor others or be self-seeking. I'm not easily angered and do not delight in evil."

"But, how can you say those things...?" sputtered the shadow as he trembled with fear and tried to regain his composure.

"I shall protect, trust, hope, and persevere." Dash looked him dead in the eye and whispered, "Because I love her."

SLAM.

The sword struck through the heart of shadowy Dash the mist dissipated, and the black crow screamed in anguish as it tried to breathe, shaking violently as it tried to catch its breath.

"You CAN'T THAY THAT!!!!" it wailed. It looked down at them as Dash helped Alex to her feet. The weakness they had felt before vanishing from their beings as light entered them.

"If I do not love, I'm nothing," said Dash. "Now get out. You have no place here."

KAWWW.

The crow beat its black wings, made its way toward the hole in the ceiling, and tried to fly away. Unfortunately for it, that was the last time it ever did anything again. True, genuine love had crippled its being. The bird fell from the air and crashed onto the ground below with a heavy THUD. Completely and utterly dead.

Alex looked into Dash's eyes and whispered, "You actually love me."

Dash smiled back at her and said, "I do."

They stood there in the tower, looking down at the gathering crowd below to view the dead bird sprawled across the ground.

"I guess our position has been compromised," said Dash with a joking shrug, and Alex laughed.

BOOM.

The walls of District 9 gave, and in an instant, the forces of Kingdom flooded the streets of District 10.

The tower began to shake violently.

"It looks like we have a way to get down now," said Alex brightly as she pointed at the hole in the ceiling.

"But how to get to it?" asked Dash as he gazed up at it for a moment.

The tower shook harder, and, in an instant, wind rushed through the hole as the ceiling of the gargantuan cavern began to get closer.

"What's happening?" asked Alex as she looked around at the shaking tower room.

"Acknowledged," said the robotic intercom. "Phase three of launch protocol has been initiated. The weapon is now airborne."

Alex and Dash looked at each other, horrified, as the cavern above them opened up, letting the rocket pass through. They flew higher and higher into the air aboard the rocket tower past District 6's maze, and through District 5's room. The frozen man saluted to them as they passed. Bursting through the ground of the marketplace and into the air.

"En route to Serenity Station," came the robotic voice. "Detonation in ten minutes."

Chapter Fourteen

The Bridge of Life

"What do we do?" cried Alex as she looked around at the interior of the massive missile.

"I don't know!" cried Dash as he flipped through the pages of the Book of Wisdom. "There's got to be something in here about this!"

Together they searched and searched through the book, but to no avail. There wasn't any information about missiles in the book.

CHOOOOOOOO.

The sounds of a steam train could be heard, and to their surprise, the Joyous Express came into view. Flying right next to the missile as the conductor leapt through the hole and into the room with Alex and Dash.

"Okay, there's been a situation," he said as he looked around at the room before them. "This thing is heading straight for our territory."

"But it doesn't pose a threat, does it?" asked Alex.

"Not to Kingdom, it doesn't," replied the conductor seriously.

"What do you mean?" asked Dash with a frown.

"This missile is heading toward the bridge between Kingdom and District 1: Serenity Station," said the conductor hastily. "If the bomb detonates there and takes the bridge out, people will no longer be able to cross into Kingdom."

"No more serenity station," whispered Alex.

"No more safe passage," said Dash.

"Exactly," replied the conductor. "Evil is trying to sever the connection between the Realm of Districts and Kingdom. If they succeed, people will no longer be able to save themselves."

"You all right down there?" cried the engineer from the express train.

"We're all right, just figuring out a plan!" called the conductor in response.

"Detonation in seven minutes," came the robotic voice.

"Shoot, that doesn't give us a lot of time," said the conductor worriedly as he nervously reached into his pocket and pulled out a map. "Let's see what we can do. Kingdom is safe because it can take a hit like this. But the bridge is held together by stone and wouldn't stand a chance."

SLAM.

The man with the mustache and bowler hat crashed through the other end of the massive missile and after seeing the three standing there, yelled, "GET OFF!"

The three stood there in horror as they gazed at the demonic man twirling his mustache as he slowly loomed over them. He glared at the conductor. "Leave us."

The conductor looked to the left, then to the right, then nodded nervously. Climbing back onto the Joyous Express and hiding in the cabin.

"So, this is your plan? To sneak aboard my rocket?" cackled the man in the mustache as he gazed at Alex and Dash with amusement. "I've seen better." He drew a massive black blade and whipped it around the shaking rocket room. "Why would you turn against me like this?"

he yelled. "I've done so. Much. For. YOU!" With every syllable, he swung the blade with more ferocity.

"You never did anything for us," grunted Alex as she slowly approached with her sword raised.

"Oh really?" growled the man as he stared at Alex in twisted disbelief. "When you needed to find shore, I told my mermaids to help you. When you wanted to wallow in your misery, I sent an icy depression to frost you. When you desired companionship with Dash in the mountain pass, I sent temptation to enhance it. When you desired a fantasy to call your own, I brought you to a shop that could provide you with such a thing!"

"But—" began Alex.

"When you felt like the road was hopeless, I provided you with options to amplify said hopelessness! What about when you were lost in the maze and wanted to get out? My Head of Security told you the answer! And when you were angry with me in District 8 and wanted to kill me, I sent a raging bear to assist with your ire." The man took a deep breath in as he thought for a moment. "I led you straight into my personal city so I could keep you in District 10 forever. So that you would have purpose in life. Everything would always be easy. Nothing challenging or difficult. Just a mindless, repetitive task you could do forever."

"Your help was nothing but a trick!" accused Dash as he pointed a finger at the man. "You're a liar and a thief. Don't pretend to be otherwise."

The man in the mustache growled and barred his teeth as he loomed closer toward them with his blade drawn. "Then you shall die for what you have done. I warned you the next time we meet, I would not be as courteous." He lunged at them, causing the flying rocket to lurch forward as the sounds of splintering wood split the rumbling.

Alex and Dash ran around the rocket room with the mustached man bearing over them with his black blade. Swinging relentlessly again and again at them, yelling about how much he had done for them and how grateful they should feel for all his supposed help.

Alex raised her sword and charged toward the man in the mustache, but black mist began to surround her. Slowly at first, but it became denser and thicker by the second, and soon she was buried in it.

"ALEX!" yelled Dash as he ran over to help her, but unfortunately, he was quickly buried in the mist as he collapsed to the ground.

"How quickly the mistakes you made stack up," whispered the man. "I do not believe we have formally been introduced. My name is Ash. I am named that because I destroy life. And just like ashes, I am the byproduct of your mistakes." He chuckled to himself as he loomed over Alex and Dash, who were now immobilized. "The weight of your own transgressions traps you," cackled Ash as he raised his sword. "A pity, isn't it? You try so hard to fight it, but deep down, you know that you are not a perfect creature. There's always a way to bait you to do something stupid."

He laughed even more as the robotic voice echoed throughout the room. "Detonation in two minutes."

Ash raised his blade, but before he could bring it down, Alex could make out a figure leaping into the room from the train. It was Peace. The one who had met her on the train before. The one who had sent on this quest.

"Peace!" roared Ash angrily as he turned his blade on the new arrival.

"Hello Ash," Peace said warmly. Light radiated in his kind eyes as he smiled at them all.

"We need help," said Alex weakly through the ash weighing her down.

"Do not be afraid," replied Peace as he looked at her kindly. "Everything is going exactly as intended."

"GET OUT," roared Ash.

"No," replied Peace calmly.

"Them I'll force you off!" snarled the man as he twirled his mustache and made a threatening step forward toward Peace.

"Turn from your evil ways and ask for forgiveness," said Peace.

"WHAT?" roared the man as he raised the long black blade above his head.

"Consider what you are about to do," said Peace. "You are about to doom yourself."

"I think not," cackled the man as he swung his blade aggressively at Peace. The kind man casually stepped out of the way just as the blade came around.

Alex and Dash held each other as they watched in horror at the events slowly unfolding. The man with the blade turned abruptly toward them and yelled, "YOU WILL NEVER ESCAPE MY HOLD ON YOU!"

He aggressively swung his blade at Peace again, missing him by inches. "Their debt will be paid in full," replied Peace as he approached Ash. "The captives will be set free."

"THEY WILL NEVER BE FREE," screamed the man, and he lunged forward and thrust the blade through Alex and Dash's mounds of ash, causing their bleeding bodies to slam into the back of the room. The wooden wall gave, and they flew out of the rocket and down toward the waters of District 1. The sounds of Peace talking to the vile man grew fainter and fainter as pain radiated through Alex's being. They were falling faster and faster toward the ocean below, and darkness shrouded them.

It felt so unfair. They had been so close, and they had failed in their mission. The bridge was about to be destroyed, and there was nothing they could do about it.

"Alex," muttered Dash weakly as he clutched his bleeding stomach.

"Yeah?" asked Alex.

"We chose the Path of Death, remember?"

Alex thought for a moment, then looked up in time to see a massive fiery explosion erupt in the distance as the rocket detonated the bridge. She watched as a figure in a bowler hat sprouted wings and flew from the scene as the column of fire rose into the air. Peace had been destroyed. That was the last thing Alex saw before the icy cold water hit her, and she was cast into darkness.

***

The explosion's echo shook the foundation of every corner of the world. It was heard from Kingdom to District 10. Every person heard that explosion, and it took many moments for everyone to realize that evil had won. Peace was no more, and darkness had won the day. Alex and Dash were dead, and there was nothing anyone could do about it.

"My friends!" announced the man in the bowler hat as he landed at the top of the overlook of District 10. "Peace is no more! You have been defeated! Surrender yourselves to me at once! The bridge connecting our lands has been detonated, and there is no way back to your King! Surrender to me now, and shall be merciful to you!" He let out a repulsive cackle and took off into the air through the massive hole the missile had flown through, filled with a twisted, sickening giddiness that didn't deserve to exist.

He flew over the oceans of District 1 and made his way over to the fallen bridge. A massive divide separates the Realm of Districts from the Light. There was only one thing left to do. He flew over to the edge of the waters, and standing at the top of an old lighthouse was Watcher. His magnifying eyes gazed at him as he approached.

"Hello, old fool," snarled the man as he twirled his mustache. "Since there is no longer a bridge for people to cross, it seems your position is no longer relevant."

"That's not true," replied Watcher as he glared at the man in the bowler hat.

"Is that so?" snapped the man as he twirled his mustache aggressively, causing a few strands to pull out. "And WHAT are you implying, old man?"

Watcher smiled at the evil before him and whispered, "You just sealed your own coffin." He chuckled and looked the man up and down. "I've been a watcher for my whole life. A family business, in fact. From parent to child. Parent to child, and one thing I have always learned is light ALWAYS cuts through darkness, but darkness cannot overwhelm light."

He casually walked over to a table and picked up a box of matches. "If even one light is present, it terrifies the dark."

"But I've won!" yelled the evil one. "I have successfully murdered the threat! Even the king cannot do anything about this! The bridge is out, and my subjects and the armies of Kingdom belong to ME."

Watcher turned toward the horizon and whispered, "You say the bridge is out?"

"I know the bridge is out! I watched it burn!"

"Then what's that?" asked Watcher slyly as he pointed toward a massive white something forming over the divide.

"WHAT?" screamed the evil one as he made his way toward the other end of the lighthouse. "BUT—"

A white bridge had formed over the chasm. Radiating with light and hope as life coursed through its strands. At once, people began to emerge from the seas of District 1. Every person who had been lost at sea began to walk out of the waters and toward the bridge of light.

"NO!" yelled the evil one as he stared in disbelief at the people, he presumed to be dead. "They all chose to die! They need to stay dead!"

Alex and Dash waved to him as they smiled and made their way toward the bridge with their friends.

"Enough of your circus act," said Watcher as he approached the evil one. "Your manipulation of people is over. Surrender."

"NO!" screamed the evil one as he gazed at Alex and Dash crossing the bridge and bathed in the light of the King. "I WILL NOT ALLOW THIS!" He drew his dark blade and flew toward the bridge at incredible speed. "STOP THAT!" he yelled as he got closer and closer. He raised the sword high above his head and dived bombed at the glowing white structure.

As soon as he came into contact with it, however, his body disintegrated and was reduced to dust. For even the evil one could not withstand the power of the King. Death had been overcome, and now the jailbreak could begin. The slaves of District 10, coming up from the waters to be made clean once again, crossing the bridge Peace's sacrifice had created. No longer serving evil but being freed through the power and authority of the Light.

Hello Again

Hey there, friend!

Now, I know what you're thinking. This was just another story about some person's life! Why should I care? I promised you this story would be different. I promised you it would be helpful. You may not have had the same adventures as I did with Dash, but one thing is that you still have time to live life to its fullest.

No matter what threats the evil one throws your way, even on the threat of death, hold fast to the Light, and He will be gracious to you. Trust in your salvation and know that He can turn your weaknesses into strengths. That's it. There is nothing left to say. I wish you well for the rest of your time in the Realm of Districts until the great prison break comes and sets the captives free.

Don't forget to live life to its fullest.

Adventures out there.

Love.

About the author

Andrew Zellgert is an award-winning surrealist author who primarily writes science fiction and fantasy for teens. He is a medalist in the Outstanding Creator Awards of Summer 2022 and has been reviewed positively by Book-Life, The Prairies Review, and Readers Favorite.

Milton Keynes UK
Ingram Content Group UK Ltd.
UKHW040656180624
444313UK00001B/17